GW00792336

Brave
Warrior

Jean Ure

For Redwings Horse Sanctuary,
Frettenham, Norwich

Scholastic Children's Books,
Commonwealth House,
1-19 New Oxford Street,
London WC1A 1NU, UK
A division of Scholastic Ltd
London ~ New York ~ Toronto ~ Sydney ~ Auckland

First published in the UK by Scholastic Ltd, 1998

Copyright © Jean Ure, 1998

ISBN 0 590 11317 8

Typeset by
Cambrian Typesetters, Frimley, Camberley, Surrey
Printed by
Cox and Wyman Ltd, Reading, Berkshire

10 9 8 7 6 5 4 3 2 1

Chapter 1

M e and my friend Jilly were learning how to ride. Horse ride; not bikes! We already knew how to ride bikes. We'd been cycling to and from school together every day for a whole year.

We'd started horse riding back in the summer holidays. It was something I'd wanted to do for ages. Being an official Animal Lover, it seemed only right that I should know about horses – but I never, ever thought I'd be able to. On account of my mum and dad being divorced, we don't have very much money. My mum works ever so hard, translating things for people from strange foreign languages such as Russian, but alas it is not very well paid.

As for my dad, Mum says he has completely lost his marbles. The reason she says this is because he gave up his very important job that he had and went to live in Cornwall with a woman called Tess*, to do his own thing. Unfortunately, doing his own thing brings in hardly any money at all, so I knew that he wouldn't be able to pay for me to have lessons.

And then a totally brilliant and unexpected thing happened. A very aged, ancient relative of Mum's went and died and she came into a windfall! Only a little-ish sort of windfall, not like people win on the lottery, but enough for me to fulfil one of my life-long ambitions.

As for Jilly, no problem there! Her dad is an airline pilot and earns simply pots. Pots and pots. And because he and Jilly's mum are also divorced, he spoils Jilly rotten. He is always giving her things. Jilly could have learnt to ride whenever she wanted. But as she said, we are best friends and it would have been disloyal to do it without me. We do things together whenever we can. That is what being best friends is all about.

Also, though I don't mean to be unfair, I think

---

* They're married now, but I didn't go to the wedding as I thought it might upset Mum.

that secretly Jilly would have been a bit too scared to do it by herself. She nearly freaked when we went to the stables the very first time and the girl who was going to teach us appeared in the yard leading this enormous black horse towards us. Jilly went, "That's not for us, is it?" and clutched at my arm. But the girl laughed and said, "No! This is Brave Warrior. He's far too big for you."

Jilly was just so relieved! But I reached up and stroked Brave Warrior's muzzle and he did the darlingest thing: he pushed his head into my hand and made this little whickering sound.

"He's a poppet," said the girl. Her name was Christy. She had long blonde hair done into a plait, and the brightest blue eyes I'd ever seen. She was only a few years older than me and Jilly, but she knew all about horses. She worked at the stables part-time in exchange for free rides. I didn't half envy her!

She told us that in spite of being so big, Warrior was one of the sweetest-natured horses you could get.

"He's a real gentleman. Aren't you, my baby?"

She pulled his head down and kissed him, right on his lovely soft nose. Jilly whispered, "He's *enormous*!"

"Just over sixteen hands," said Christy. "Not as tall as some. Some of the hunters can go up to seventeen. That's *really* huge."

I could see that even sixteen was quite huge enough for Jilly. But I wasn't scared!

"Will we be able to ride him one day?" I said.

Christy laughed and said, "Not until you've grown a bit! But you could probably just walk round the field on him, once you've learnt the basics."

I would have given anything to walk round the field on him right there and then! I was quite disappointed when Christy put him in his stall and brought out two little ponies for us. Jilly said, "Oh! That's better!" but Christy must have seen that I was still hankering after Warrior. She said, "Don't you worry! One of these is a right little tear-away. He'll give you a run for your money."

Jilly turned pale at that. She said, "Wh-which one?"

"Jet." Christy pointed to the little stubby black one. He was standing there looking as if butter

4

wouldn't melt in his mouth, but I noticed that he had a naughty glint in his eye!

"He's not vicious," said Christy. "In fact, he's quite a comedian. But he'll take advantage, if you let him. And he's strong, although he's small. Cherokee, now, she's a lady. She'll do what she's told. Far better behaved, aren't you?" And she put an arm round Cherokee's neck and hugged her. "OK! Who wants which?"

Jilly looked at me, pleadingly. She is taller than I am, so by rights she should have had Jet. He was taller than Cherokee by about half a hand. But Jet had that wicked glint in his eye! Cherokee was a lady. She was pretty and pink. Jilly is also pretty and pink, whereas I am quite dark and what Mum calls "sallow". I am certainly not beautiful, and neither was Jet. He was too stocky, with a thick neck and a shaggy coat. But so what? What do looks matter?

"I'll have Jet," I said.

Jilly was really grateful. And she looked so good, mounted on Cherokee, both of them so pink and pretty, that I really didn't mind – even though Jet was a handful! Christy told me that

5

she thought we'd made the right choices, as I seemed to have more confidence than Jilly.

"You've got a really good seat. You should do well."

I didn't tell Jilly, natch! I didn't want to put her off or to sound like I was boasting. But it made me feel quite proud 'cos I'd wanted to learn how to ride for *such* a long time.

The first few lessons we had to stay in the ring, just learning how to hold the reins and how to sit properly – straight back, with arms tucked in and heels down.

"Down, down! Heels *down*!" Christy kept shouting.

"I can't!" wailed Jilly. Her toes kept going down, instead. "I think there's something wrong with my feet!"

"There's nothing wrong with your feet," said Christy. "Watch Clara – see how she does it!"

"Heels *down*!" I chanted to Jilly, as we rode on our bicycles to and from the stables.

"I don't think I'll ever get the hang of it," moaned Jilly.

"You will!" I said. I said it quite fiercely. I

didn't want to go riding on my own! Best friends do things together. "Oh, please, Jilly! Don't give up! After all," I said, "if you're going to be a vet" (which she is) "you *need* to know about horses."

One day when we went for our lesson, Christy said she thought the time had come for us to try going on a real ride. I was thrilled! Jilly, needless to say, was a bit apprehensive.

"Do you really think we're ready for it?" she quavered.

"Absolutely!" Christy nodded. "You can't stay stuck in the ring for ever, you'll get bored. So will the horses!"

A voice suddenly spoke at us from one of the stalls.

"I don't know what you're panicking for. A *baby* couldn't fall off Cherokee. She's like an arm-chair."

We froze. We knew that voice! It belonged to Puffin Portinari, a particularly horrible girl in our class at school. Me and Jilly called her No-Neck, for obvious reasons: she hasn't got one!

"This is Puffin," said Christy. "Do you know each other?"

Glumly, we admitted that we did.

"She's joining us on the ride."

My heart went *clunk*, right down to my boots, which in fact weren't boots at all but just mouldy ordinary shoes. Our mums had said they weren't going to fork out for expensive riding gear until we'd been doing it long enough to be quite sure that we wanted to go on doing it. So in the meantime we had to wear shoes and jeans and anoraks and borrow hard hats from the ones that were kept at the stables.

It was very belittling – especially when we looked at old No-Neck in her smart tweedy jacket, her stretchy riding breeches and her long shiny boots. *And* she had a superior blue hat. The stable hats were just ordinary black ones, all battered and bashed.

"I don't know how you can bear to wear hats that other people have worn," said No-Neck. "Ugh! The thought of it makes me squirm!"

Very pointedly we ignored her and went off to saddle our horses, or ponies, actually. We had learnt that Cherokee was part Welsh pony and Jet was an Exmoor, which was why he was a bit –

well, basic. Exmoor ponies are almost the same as they were in prehistoric days. That is going back quite a long time!

Of course, old No-Neck had her own pony, didn't she? Beautiful and golden with a creamy mane and tail. No-Neck said she was a palomino.

"Daddy bought her for my birthday. She's worth ever such a lot of money."

You can see why No-Neck is not one of our favourite people. I mean, anyone who can boast that their pony is worth a lot of money! If I had a pony I wouldn't care *what* it was worth. I wouldn't care if it wasn't worth anything at all. I would still love it and look after it. And I would never, *ever* sell it on. I hate the way people do that. Oh, they say, I have grown out of this pony, I need something bigger, I need something better. If I were ever lucky enough to have a pony of my own, it would be for LIFE.

Unless, perhaps, it went to a sanctuary – say, if I ran out of money and could no longer afford to look after it. But not just to sell it on, when for all you know it could end up as *horse meat*.

I wasn't thinking of horse meat, that day me

and Jilly went for our first ride. I was too busy being happy! There were just the four of us, me and Jilly, Christy and No-Neck. Christy was riding Brave Warrior. I'd never seen him out before. He was the most beautiful, beautiful horse! Shiny and glossy and really intelligent. Christy said she only had to touch him and he would respond.

"I almost only have to *think*."

"That's what you can do with a really good horse," said No-Neck. And she turned and stared disdainfully at me and Jilly on Jet and Cherokee. I felt quite indignant on Jet's behalf! I'd become quite fond of that funny little chunky pony.

"Jet will do anything I ask him," I said; and I touched him with my heels, the way we'd been taught in the ring, and sure enough he broke into a trot!

I said, "Good boy, Jet! Good boy!" and he tossed his shaggy head and stepped out ever so proudly. Up-down, up-down, up-down. And I went up-down with him! Rising to the trot! It was the most incredible and amazing feeling.

If you *don't* rise to the trot, it is really

uncomfortable. And if the horse is going up-down while you are going down-up – well! That is a recipe for disaster. At the very least it will result in a *sore bum*.

That is what was happening to poor old Jilly. She just couldn't get the rhythm right! I saw her bouncing about on top of the saddle and I felt for her, I truly did, but I was just so . . . exhilarated! I squeezed with my thighs and urged Jet to trot even faster, trit-trot, trit-trot, trit-trot, his little stumpy legs smashing up and down, with old No-Neck's palomino, who was called Caramel, swishing her tail in his face as we moved up the lane.

"You OK, Jilly?" called Christy; and Jilly called back, "Just about!" which I thought was really brave of her.

At the end of the lane we reached a flat piece of land which is known to local horse riders as the Gallops, where, if you are experienced, you can go flat out.

"Can we gallop, can we gallop?" demanded No-Neck. "Let's go!"

"*No.*" Christy caught hold of Caramel's bridle. "Jilly and Clara aren't ready for that."

"I could gallop," I said.

It was so selfish of me! I wasn't thinking about poor Jilly at all. But anyway, Christy was very firm. She said there would be *no galloping* on this ride.

Needless to say, No-Neck fell into the most tremendous sulk and started grumbling about "having to come out with beginners".

"It isn't any fun at all!"

"You didn't have come if you didn't want to," said Christy. "You know perfectly well they've only just started riding. And anyway, Warrior can't gallop. You just fall in behind me and hold that horse back. We may do a bit of gentle cantering later on, when we get to the field."

Old No-Neck muttered, but did as she was told. She reined in next to me and mumbled something about horses not being used if they couldn't do what was expected of them.

"Are you talking about Warrior?" I said. I'd thought it odd when Christy said he couldn't gallop. A big beautiful horse like that!

No-Neck thwacked petulantly at Caramel's neck with the reins. "He ought to be pensioned off!"

"Why?" I said. "Is he old?"

"His lungs are damaged. He isn't any use any more."

"Oh!" I stared at her, in dismay. "Oh, poor Warrior! How did it happen?"

"He was in a fire. Only no one told the stupid person that bought him and she didn't bother to get him checked out, so he was just a *total* waste of money. Which is why the owner's done a bunk and Mrs Hart is stuck with him."

Mrs Hart was the woman who ran the stables. She was quite good-looking but rather hatchet-faced. I was always glad that it was Christy who was teaching us to ride and not her! I think she would have freaked Jilly out completely.

"Why did his owner do a bunk?" I said.

"'Cos she liveried him here, and when—"

"She did what?" I said.

"*Liveried* him." No-Neck gave me this withering glance. I could tell she was thinking, these non-horsey people are just so ignorant! But there was no call for her to be all superior. Everyone has to learn.

"What does liveried mean?" I said.

"It means, like. . ." No-Neck flapped a hand, impatiently. "Board and lodging. The stables look after the horse and feed it and the owner pays them. So as soon as this person discovered she'd bought a knackered horse, she did a bunk. Right?"

I nodded, doubtfully.

"Well, I mean, she couldn't sell him on 'cos he's not worth anything. All he can do is just trundle about. He's totally useless!"

"Won't his lungs get better?" I said.

"No. They're shot."

I didn't ask her what she meant by shot. I guessed she meant that alas they had been ruined for all time.

"He's so beautiful!" I said.

"Yes, and he just stands about all day, eating his head off. All they can do with him is take him out on beginner rides. It's so *frustrating*!"

No-Neck slapped at Caramel with the reins. Caramel twitched, and jumped. I could tell she really wanted to go.

"We usually *fly* along this bit!"

"It's not Warrior's fault," I said.

14

"I know it's not his *fault*. But they oughtn't to be using him!"

No-Neck went whisking off, all self-important, to join Christy at the front. I hauled on the reins – you had to haul, with Jet. He was a really tough little guy – and waited for Jilly to catch up with me.

"Did you know about Warrior?" I said. "It's so sad!"

I told her about his lungs and how he couldn't gallop, and Jilly said, "I don't see that it matters so long as he can still walk and trot. I mean, who *wants* to gallop, anyway?"

But she agreed with me that it was terrible for such a big, beautiful horse to be so handicapped.

"It's worse than Mud being deaf."

Mud is our dog, Jilly's and mine, that we rescued. He was the one who started us off being Animal Lovers. It is horrid for a dog to be deaf, but I think it is even horrider for a horse to have damaged lungs. Horses are intended by nature to gallop and canter.

We did a little bit of cantering in Stiles Farm field, but even that didn't satisfy No-Neck. She went careering off on Caramel before Christy could stop her. Poor Warrior desperately wanted to go after him, but Christy held him back. I *tried* to hold Jet, but he was too strong. He lit out after Caramel as if a whole herd of tigers were behind us! It was a bit frightening, actually; I really thought I was going to come off. But I didn't! I hung on and hung on, even though I slipped half out of the saddle and ended up losing the reins and clutching for dear life at his mane. I was quite pleased with myself!

Christy was furious. She tore strips off No-Neck. She gave her this long lecture on BAD MANNERS and LACK OF CONSIDERATION. She said, "If Clara had broken her neck, it would have been all your fault!"

Good little Cherokee had behaved perfectly, which was just as well as Jilly told me afterwards that she would have been terrified.

"Weren't you?" she said. "Just a little bit?"

"No way," I told her. "It was exciting!"

Well, I didn't want to put her off. No point admitting I'd nearly had a heart attack!

When we got back to the stables we put our

ponies away and removed their tack (which is the horsey term for the saddle and the bridle), then we gave them their carrots and rushed off to see Warrior. Although we loved Jet and Cherokee, Warrior was our favourite. He was everyone's favourite! A great big spoilt darling.

But he was so kind and sweet and gentle. One time, for instance, when I was helping muck out, he went and stood on my foot with one of his huge, slab-like hooves. Some horses, if they do that, will just go on standing there while your foot slowly *c-r-u-n-c-h-e-s* beneath their weight. You really have to shove at them to get them off. But Warrior knew what he'd done immediately. I didn't even have to yell. I mean, I *did* yell! You bet I did! But he'd already lifted his hoof and moved it away. And he never bit or kicked or tried to crush you against the side of the stall, which is what some of them did if they got a bit mean. So we always went to say goodbye to him and give him something special, like a nice juicy apple.

Christy was still with him. She'd hung his saddle over the door and was rubbing him down.

"Why is he all wet?" asked Jilly.

"He's sweated a bit," said Christy. "It's not good to leave them like that."

"The others didn't sweat," I said. It wasn't a specially warm day and the ride had only been a beginner's one, not a mad dash about the countryside. "Is it because of his lungs?"

"I'm afraid so." Christy blew softly up Warrior's nostrils. She had told us that horses like you to do that. It was a way of communicating with them. "He has to be taken great care of, don't you, my gentle giant?"

"But so long as he's looked after," said Jilly, "he'll be all right?"

"Well – yes."

Christy didn't sound terribly certain.

"He won't get any *worse*?" I said.

"Not if he's treated properly. He really needs to retire. He needs to live in a meadow! He shouldn't have to go on working. He's been through such a lot! Can you imagine how it must feel to be a horse, shut up in a box, with fire roaring all about you? It must have been absolutely terrifying for him!"

18

Jilly stroked Warrior's neck. I reached up and gave him his apple and put my finger in his big rubbery lower lip and wobbled it about. For some reason, he seemed to enjoy it when I did that!

"What will happen to him?" said Jilly.

"I don't know." Christy snatched the saddle off the top of the door. "Don't ask me. I don't want to think about it!"

That was all she would say. She wouldn't talk to us any more.

Worriedly, we walked across to the Office to pay for our ride. I suppose we could have asked Mrs Hart what was going to happen to Warrior, but she was such a cross-looking, barking sort of person that we didn't like to. It was No-Neck who told us. She came running out to join us as we went to fetch our bikes.

"Christy doesn't like talking about Warrior. It upsets her."

"Why?" said Jilly.

"'Cos he's going to the knacker's," said No-Neck. "He's going to be made into horse meat."

Chapter 2

Jilly and me couldn't believe it! We thought it was some kind of a joke. A *sick* joke. But No-Neck is a sick person. She goes fox hunting and thinks it's all right for people to wear fur. She is truly disgusting.

"Ask Mrs Hart if you don't believe me," she said. "She'll tell you. She's sending him for horse meat."

The way she said it made me go cold. That big, soft, gentle boy was going to have his life taken from him, and No-Neck couldn't have cared less!

Horsey people can sometimes be very hard. I have noticed this.

"It's no use crying over what can't be helped," said No-Neck. "It's how they'll all end up, probably."

20

"*What?*" We stared at her, horrified.

"All of them." She flapped a hand towards the stables. "When they can't be used any more. What else can you do with them?"

"Keep them!" I said.

Jilly didn't say anything. I think that for once she was just too flabbergasted. As a rule, she is really good at holding her own with low-life dregs such as No-Neck.

"Keep them where?" said No-Neck.

"In a field!"

"Doing what?"

"Not doing anything! Just enjoying their retirement!"

Jilly suddenly found her tongue.

"Old people retire! Why can't horses?"

"Some do," said No-Neck. "If their owners can afford it. But you can't if you're running a business."

No-Neck's dad is a farmer and so she is used to innocent animals being dragged off to the slaughter house. She doesn't see anything wrong in it. She thinks people like me and Jilly are just stupid and sentimental.

"You have to be realistic," she said. "That's your trouble! You're just so *stupid* and *sentimental*. Animals are only animals."

"They have feelings!" I said.

"Not like we do. Anyway, we're the top species."

"That doesn't mean we have to go round killing everything!"

"No," said Jilly. "It means we have a duty to look after them."

"We do look after them, while they're alive," said No-Neck.

"Well, you couldn't very well look after them when they're dead!" I retorted.

"I didn't mean that!" Old No-Neck had gone all red and blotchy. She always goes red when she argues with me and Jilly. It's because she can't ever get the better of us. Cruelty is cruelty, and that's all there is to it.

"What I mean, what I *meant*," she said, "was that a horse is a working animal. You can't afford to go on feeding them if they're not earning their keep."

Which was something, I bet, she'd got from her dad.

22

Heatedly, Jilly said, "Horses weren't put on this earth to earn money for human beings!"

"How do you know?" said No-Neck. That is the sort of childish thing she always resorts to saying.

"Well, I don't," said Jilly, "but you don't, either. We don't actually know why *any* of us were put on this earth –" she was really getting into her stride by now! – "so it seems to me, if we're so superior, we ought to be taking care of other species, not just using them to make money for us and then foully killing them when they're too old."

"Or too sick," I added. I always do my best to support Jilly whenever I can, though I am not as clever at arguing as she is.

"There ought to be a law against it," I said. "Everybody that owns a horse should be made to sign something saying they'll let it retire when it can't work any more."

"A pension fund for horses!"

"Yes, like human beings have."

"And rest homes –"

"Rest fields –"

"Where they could all live together and be happy and just noddy about doing their own thing."

"That is what *ought* to happen," I said.

"Oh, get real!" snapped No-Neck. "Stupid townies!"

She calls us that because she has always lived in the country and thinks herself superior. She will probably still be saying it when we are old and wizened and haven't set foot in a town for nigh on fifty years. *If* we're still on speaking terms, which most probably we shan't be. With any luck, a herd of maddened cows will have run her over and crushed her, long before that.

A big flash car had pulled up in the yard. No-Neck went stalking over to it.

"Good riddance," muttered Jilly.

"Do you think –" I fiddled miserably with the handlebars on my bike, rolling the rubber hand grips up and down – "do you think it's true what she said? About Warrior?"

There was a silence. I thought that Jilly wasn't going to reply, but then she burst out, "It's not fair! He couldn't help his lungs being damaged!"

"No," I agreed, "it was human b[

"And now they're going to kill h[

I drew a long, quivering breath[

really, we ought to go and ask Mrs H[

We most desperately didn't want ʋ. I mean, for one thing we were a bit scared of her; and for another, as long as we didn't hear it *officially* we could still go on pretending that No-Neck had just been making up stories to alarm us.

But Jilly agreed with me that we had to do it.

We propped our bicycles against the side of the tack room and trailed back into the stables. Mrs Hart was in the caravan that she used as an office. She was adding things up on a calculator. Working out how much all her horses were earning before she sent them off to the knacker's yard.

I suddenly came over all bold and defiant and rapped quite smartly at the door. We were Animal Lovers! Nobody scared us!

Mrs Hart looked up and saw us.

"Yes," she said. "What can I do for you?"

The words came blurting out of me: "We want to know if it's true about Brave Warrior?"

obably didn't sound very polite, but I
asn't feeling polite. I was feeling ...
pugnacious!

Mrs Hart, all icy, said, "Is what true?"

"That he's going to be turned into horse meat!"

I know it's silly, because however intelligent
horses are – and they *are* – they can't understand
human language. All the same, I felt really guilty
saying a thing like that in Warrior's hearing.

I could see that Mrs Hart didn't like being
questioned. I expect she considered it an
impertinence. She said, "I know it's unpleasant,
none of us enjoy it, but we do not live in a perfect
world and I am not a charity institution. I have a
business to run. He's not my horse, I didn't buy
him. I'm just the poor fool who's left to pick up
the tab."

"But what about Warrior?" I pleaded.

Surely she must have *some* feelings for him?

"For your information," said Mrs Hart, "I have
been paying for his food and keep for the past
three months. I cannot go on indefinitely. If the
person who bought him had had the sense to get
him checked over by a vet before parting with her

money – well! He'd probably have gone to the knackers there and then, so at least he's had a few more months of life. Now, if you'll excuse me, I'm busy."

Jilly and I walked miserably away. Our footsteps carried us round to the other side of the indoor ring, to Warrior's box. His big horsey head was hanging over the door. I put my finger in his lower lip and wobbled it for him. Jilly was busy with her handkerchief.

"He's so trusting!" she wept.

It is truly terrible the way that animals place their trust in human beings, only to be let down. To be herded into wagons and driven to their deaths. To be locked in cages and tortured. To be clubbed and shot and brutally kicked. I think wild animals are sensible to keep away from us. I would!

Christy had seen Jilly weeping into her handkerchief. She came over to us and said, "I suppose Puffin told you?"

I nodded. I knew that if I tried to say anything I would probably start weeping, too.

"It's not Pippa's fault." Pippa was Mrs Hart.

Honestly! She didn't look in the least like a Pippa. More like a . . . a *Gertrude*, or a Helga.

"It's his owner," said Christy. "Dumping him on us! She's the one to blame. You don't think Pippa likes having to send a horse to the knacker's?"

"Then why does she do it?" sobbed Jilly.

"She's been trying not to. She's kept putting it off. But sooner or later—"

"It's so cruel!" I said.

"It's life," said Christy, sadly.

"You mean, *death*!" shouted Jilly.

We just couldn't accept it. We had become Animal Lovers to fight for all those poor defenceless creatures who couldn't fight for themselves. We couldn't let Brave Warrior go for horse meat!

On the way home we met our neighbour, Mr Hennessy, taking his dog Dixie for a walk. Mr Hennessy was one of our favourite people. He lived in the first cottage in our lane and Jilly and me were secretly hoping that he and my mum might some day become An Item. It was only a short time since she'd stopped seeing Beastly

28

Bernard (a disgusting creep that went fox hunting and thought rabbits were for shooting) so perhaps it was still a bit too soon. But we could dream!

The minute she saw us, Dixie came wambling up, all happy and wagging. She couldn't give us a proper doggy greeting and lick us because she's a pit bull terrier and sadly has to wear a muzzle all the time she is out of doors as that is the law. If she is found without a muzzle, she could be taken away and destroyed. And yet she is not at all a fierce dog. She is a big softie! Even if she does have teeth like a shark.

"Hi, you two!" Mr Hennessy waved a hand. "You're looking a bit plum duff."

We giggled, in spite of ourselves.

"What's plum duff?"

"Plum duff, rough. What's the problem?"

I sighed. Jilly plucked at her handkerchief.

"Oh, dear! Don't tell me ... more animal trouble?"

Mr Hennessy knew all about me and Jilly being Animal Lovers. It was because of us that he had adopted Dixie. He had also helped us rescue a little fox that we had befriended.

"Let me guess! You've just been to the stables and . . . something bad has happened to a horse?"

"Not yet," I said, "but it's going to!" And I told him about Brave Warrior and his damaged lungs and how he was going to be sent to the knackers to be turned into horse meat.

Mr Hennessy was really sympathetic. He always is. That is why he is one of our favourite people! Our mums have this tendency to groan and say, "Not *again*?" They are glad we are not obsessed with boys or make-up or clothes, but they do sometimes get a bit tired of our great passion for animals.

"This girl," I said, "that goes to our school, she said –" a huge wave of despondency suddenly came over me – "she said that most horses end up as horse meat!"

Gravely, Mr Hennessy agreed that that was "the downside" of going riding.

"If you own your own horse, fine. But I'm afraid it's true that an awful lot of riding school neddies are just slung on to the rubbish tip the minute they get past it. It's one of the hard facts of life . . . you can't rescue 'em all."

Jilly blotched rather fiercely at her eyes. "Just because we can't rescue them all, doesn't mean we shouldn't try to rescue any!"

"True," said Mr Hennessy. "Very true. Why don't you ask your friend at the Sanctuary. Meg. See if she can suggest anything."

Meg is another of our favourite people. She runs a sanctuary called End of the Line, where sometimes we help out. It's where Mr Hennessy got Dixie from.

"Give her a go," said Mr Hennessy. "Why not?"

Mr Hennessy and Dixie went walking on. Jilly and me looked at each other.

"We're *always* asking Meg," I said.

"I know," said Jilly, "but what else can we do? She knows more than we do! We're still learning."

"Yes, and it is for animals," I said.

"Let's do it!" said Jilly.

We had to race home first to tell our mums, otherwise they would have started to flap and wring their hands and say, "Where can they have got to?" And then they would think we had fallen

31

off our bikes and broken our necks, which is the sort of thing that mums always seem to think you are doing. (If you are not falling off and breaking your neck, you are riding your bicycle beneath the wheels of a container truck and being decapitated, or jumping into cars with strange men, or skating about on frozen bottomless lakes and drowning yourself. A mum's life is *full* of worry. I am never going to be one!)

I didn't tell Mum why we were going to see Meg. I didn't want her groaning! And fortunately she was in the middle of a rush job, which is what she calls a translation that has to be done in a simply stupendous hurry, so all she said was, "Don't be too long, you've got to take Mud out."

"I'll do it when I come back!" I yelled.

We whizzed along to End of the Line in record time, only to discover that Meg wasn't there. Denise, who is her assistant, said that she had gone off on a sponsored walk, all the way to Wales, to try and raise some money.

"Funds are really low. We're getting desperate."

Our hearts plummeted when she said that.

"Why can't they give lottery money to animal charities?" wailed Jilly. "Instead of always to people?"

"That'll be the day," said Denise. "Anyway, what can I do for you?"

"Nothing, I don't expect." I said it glumly.

"We wondered if you'd have room for another horse," said Jilly.

Denise sucked in her breath. "Not a chance! We can barely feed the ones we've got. Unless, maybe, it's a Shetland pony?"

I heaved a sigh and said no, it was a big, beautiful horse and it was going to be turned into horse meat if we couldn't find some way of rescuing it.

"There's a horse sanctuary over Spindle Down," said Denise. "You could try them. I'm not sure of their number, but they'll be in the book. They might be able to help. And look, while you're here, you wouldn't feel like exercising some of the dogs for us, would you?"

We can never resist an appeal to exercise the poor abandoned dogs at End of the Line. Even though we had to exercise our very own dog when we got back home, we spent an hour in the field throwing a ball and running and chasing. It's all part of being an Animal Lover.

By the time we arrived back it was too late to ring the horse sanctuary, but we got the number from Directory Enquiries. Unfortunately, Mum heard us doing it. Guess what? She groaned!

"Not *again*?" she said. "I can't bear it!"

"Bear what?" I said.

"All the heartache and the breast beating and you and Jilly in floods of tears and wanting me to keep turkeys in the kitchen and wombats in the garden, and—"

"Mum, I have *never* wanted you to keep a wombat in the garden!" I said.

"You wanted me to keep a turkey in the kitchen!"

"Only for one night." Then he'd gone to Hen Haven. It hadn't been much to ask, had it? A turkey in the kitchen for just *one night*?

Mum said, "Well! I'm not having a horse out there."

Sadly, I said that a garden our size would be far too small for a horse like Warrior.

"Good," said Mum.

"It's not good!" I said. "His life is at stake!"

"Clara, please don't," said Mum. "I have lived through this with kittens, I have lived through it with a donkey, I have lived through it with a fox—"

"And now it's a horse!" I said. "And we're going to rescue him!"

I have *explained* to Mum – I have told her over and over – that me and Jilly have dedicated ourselves to rescuing animals. She can't expect us to just rescue one or two and then stop. It is a *lifetime's commitment*. You have to be prepared for a bit of heartache.

Oh, but lying in bed that night, with Mud snuggled up beside me, I had more than just a bit of heartache. I had nightmares. I kept imagining poor darling Warrior being dragged away to the knacker's yard, terrified, not knowing what was happening, smelling all the blood and the fear . . . maybe even being put on a boat and taken off to France to be slaughtered over there. I knew about these things. Jilly and me had signed petitions. The poor frightened horses, crammed into the dark holds of the cross-channel ferries, sometimes without any water, sometimes in agony with broken legs. And then, at the end of the journey, rough horrible men pushing them and pulling them, shouting at them, hitting them, forcing them towards their death.

There is so much cruelty in this world! You don't realize it when you are very young.

I cuddled close to Mud and vowed that next morning we would ring the horse sanctuary. Our gentle giant was not going to end his days in pain and fear. Not if me and Jilly had anything to do with it.

Chapter 3

Next day was Monday, and we had to go to school. School is *such* a nuisance! Always getting in the way of things you want to do. Such as, for instance, ringing the horse sanctuary.

"Mum, I've got to!" I cried.

"Not at this hour of the morning," said Mum. "Look at the time! You'll be late for school."

Late for school! What did late for school matter? Warrior's life was a stake!

I said this to Mum and she said, "Clara, we've had all this out before. Your school work comes first. *After* school is the time for rescuing animals."

"But it might be too late by then! Mum, *please*! Let me ring before I go!"

She wouldn't, of course. They have this absolute *obsession* about school. Like if you just miss half an hour of it your entire life will be a disaster and you'll end up in a cardboard box, holding out a begging bowl.

I really envy those kids that go bunking off all the time. I don't know how they get away with it! I only have to be five seconds late and Mum starts going raving demented.

"Come along, Clara!" she said. "Don't keep Jilly waiting."

"But, *Mum*—"

"Clara, I'm warning you!"

"I suppose you couldn't do it?" I said.

"Do what?"

"Ring the sanctuary!"

"Oh, for goodness' sake!" said Mum. "As if I haven't got enough on my plate! Why can't the people at the stables do it, if they're so bothered?"

I'd never though of that. Why *couldn't* they? I guessed because Mrs Hatchet Face didn't really care, in spite of what she said. She just wanted to get rid of poor Warrior the quickest way possible. But Christy cared! Why couldn't she have rung the sanctuary?

I must have been looking despondent because all of a sudden Mum relented.

"All right, all right!" she said. "I'll do it! If it's going to set your mind at rest. *I will do it.*"

"Oh, Mum! Thank you!" I rushed at her and hugged her. She is a mum in a million! "You know what you've got to say?"

"Tell me," said Mum.

"You've got to say that there's this darling beautiful horse that's got damaged lungs because of being in a fire and if someone doesn't rescue him he's going to the knacker's yard!"

"So you want them to come and take him away?"

"*Yes!*" I nodded, vigorously.

"Leave it with me," said Mum. "I'll see what I can do. You just get off to school and stop worrying."

I got off to school but I couldn't stop worrying. I said to Jilly, "Why couldn't Christy have rung the sanctuary?"

Jilly agreed it was a puzzle. After all, Christy loved Warrior as much as we did. She couldn't bear the thought of him going for horse meat.

"People just seem to let things happen," said

Jilly, sadly. "Like where we lived before, we knew this woman who had two dogs and she was going to Australia, so guess what she did? She had the dogs put down 'cos she couldn't think what else to do with them."

I stared at her, shocked. "That's disgraceful!"

"I know," said Jilly. "But it's what people do. They just can't be bothered."

Like Christy. It had probably never even occurred to her to ring up a sanctuary.

"It takes a lot of effort," said Jilly.

I said, "Tell me about it!" And then I added that was all the more reason for people like her and me to be Animal Lovers. "'Cos we're *prepared* to make the effort."

It was only our second week back at school after the summer holidays. We had a new class teacher, Mr O'Shea, that all the girls were swooning over. Well, all except me and Jilly. We had turned our backs on men. We simply didn't have the time.

"All this drooling and dribbling," said Jilly. "They could be out there rescuing animals!"

Old No-Neck and her best mate Geraldine

Hooper were two of the main droolers. They'd already tattooed PO'S on their arms in felt tip pen. The P stood for Paul, which was Mr O'Shea's first name. I don't know how they discovered.

Geraldine said loftily, "We have ways of finding out."

Soppily went and asked him, I bet.

"Please, sir, what does the P stand for, sir? Is it Peter, sir? Is it Patrick, sir? Oh, sir, please, sir, tell us what it stands for, sir!"

"He looks just like Brad Pitt," simpered No-Neck.

I said, "Who's Brad *Pitt* when he's at home?" and Geraldine and No-Neck gave these exaggerated sighs and rolled their eyes around in their eye sockets.

"He's a film star, *dummy*!"

"I've never heard of him," I said.

"Neither have I," said Jilly.

"That's because all you ever think about is *animals*!"

"Yes, and we're thinking about one right now!" said Jilly. "About a poor horse with damaged lungs that people want to *murder*."

"Oh, heavens!" Geraldine covered her ears with her hands. "She's off again!"

"They're just so *stupid* and *sentimental*," said No-Neck.

"Why do they only care about animals? Far worse things happen to human beings."

"Human beings aren't murdered just because they're sick!" retorted Jilly.

Of course they ignored that. They always ignore things when they haven't got an answer.

"Think of all those poor starving *people*," said Geraldine.

"Yes," gushed No-Neck. "All those poor starving little children in—"

And then she stopped, 'cos she couldn't think where it was they were starving. That was because she didn't really *care*. She was just saying it to needle us.

"There's nothing we can do to help the starving children," said Jilly.

"Yes, there is! You could give all your money to Oxfam instead of wasting it on animals!"

"Do you give all your money to Oxfam?" said Jilly.

Oh, brilliant! That stumped them. Geraldine turned bright scarlet. No-Neck snapped, "I do when I can!"

"You do when you *can*? That doesn't make any sense!" said Jilly. "You either *do* give all your money, or you *don't* give all your money. And if you *don't* give all your money—"

"You can jolly well just shut up!" I finished.

I get so sick of people telling me and Jilly that we ought to be helping human beings instead of animals. Like human beings are just *so* much more important. And anyway, all these people, what do they do? Nothing! They just have a go at me and Jilly. It absolutely annoys me.

Which is why I told Geraldine and No-Neck that they could jolly well shut up and why they told me to go boil myself and next thing I knew we'd all got into this rebarbative slanging match, with insults flying across the room and bouncing off the walls.

I like that word, *rebarbative*. I don't only think about animals! I read books, as well. So sucks to Geraldine Hooper.

Anyway, Mr O'Shea came into the room just in time to hear No-Neck screaming, "Pig's bum, you abject *idiot*!" which I thought served her right.

Mr O'Shea, in his lovely Irish accent, said, "I'll pretend I didn't hear that," and No-Neck turned bright red from head to foot like some kind of human pillar box. She even had her mouth open! I felt like posting my maths book in it.

Jilly and I thought about Warrior all day long. I kept wondering if Mum had telephoned yet, and if so, what the horse sanctuary had said. They might even have sent a horsebox and rescued him already!

"I'd hate not seeing him again," said Jilly, "but I wouldn't mind if it meant he was safe."

"We could always go and visit," I said. "Spindle Down isn't that far. I bet Mr Hennessy would take us."

All we wanted to do at the end of school was to go rushing home. Instead, we had to stay on for a boring old rehearsal for the boring old end-of-term show. Well, it wasn't really boring. It was all about the Children's Crusade and me and Jilly were part of it. Part of the Crusade, I mean. So was everybody else in our class! We didn't get to say anything; we just did a bit of marching and milling about and sang a few songs.

Normally I would quite have enjoyed it, even though I can't sing for toffee. Geraldine Hooper kept hissing, "You're *flat*!" and screwing up her face like she was in agony. Ha! Maybe she was. Maybe my voice is my secret weapon. I could just go and *sing* into her ear whenever I want to annoy her. But I didn't really feel like singing, that afternoon. I felt like racing back home and discovering that Warrior had been saved!

It was half-past five when me and Jilly got back. Jilly had to be straight in for her tea.

"Let me know what's happened!" she said.

I went tearing in through the back door. Mud immediately hurled himself at me, and so did Benjy, my little brother. Mud barked, and Benjy shouted, "Dub dodda dode dar!"

"Mud got a gold star?" I said. Benjy is deaf (like Mud) and when he's excited he gabbles. "What did he get a gold star for?"

"Codda learnda dit when I ded dit!"

"He learned to sit. That's brilliant!" I said.

But I wasn't really interested in Mud learning

to sit. Not just at that moment. I wanted to find out about Warrior!

"Mum?" I pushed past Mud and Benjy and went through into the hall. "Mum, did you ring? What did they say? Are they going to take him?"

"Oh!" Mum sprang round from her desk. Her hand flew to her mouth.

"Oh, my goodness, Clara! I'm so sorry! I clean forgot!"

"*Mum!*" I wailed.

"Oh, Clara, I'm sorry, I really am! I tried them this morning and they were engaged, and then Mr Hennessy came round and we had a coffee, and then I got in a panic about this wretched translation . . . I've just been working ever since!"

I couldn't get mad at her. It's not very often that Mum lets me down. And she was so apologetic! She obviously felt bad about it. All the same, it was a bitter blow.

"Try them now," said Mum.

I did, but of course they weren't there. It was too late.

"I'll do it first thing tomorrow," said Mum. "I will, I promise!"

"Yes," I said. I swallowed. "All right."

"Wodge, wodge!" Benjy was clutching at my sleeve. "Wodge wod Dub dud! Dub, *did*." He pointed sternly at the floor. "Dub, *did*. Dub, did *DOWD*."

Mud did sit, in the end – but only after Benjy had exerted all his strength and pushed at his bum! And then he immediately sprang back up again, grinning and wagging; whereupon Benjy, the great dog trainer, gave him a dog biscuit and praised him lavishly!

"*Dood* dod, *dood* dod!"

"Yeah, that's great," I said. "I'm really impressed."

"Dow you!" said Benjy; but I wasn't in the mood for training Mud.

"I'd better ring Jilly," I said.

"Tell her I'm wearing sack cloth and ashes," said Mum.

Whatever that meant. I think it meant that she was truly repentant.

Jilly came to the phone all bubbly and eager and full of hope.

"Clara! What happened?"

I felt terrible, having to break the news, but Jilly was really brave about it.

"Oh. Well—" I heard the sound of gulping, which I think was because she was eating her tea. Though it may have been a lump in her throat. "I suppose she couldn't help it. It doesn't mean as much to her as it does to us. She doesn't know Warrior."

"She's promised to ring tomorrow," I said.

"If he's still alive."

"Oh, Jilly, don't!" I begged.

"Maybe you ought to ring the stables," said Jilly. "You could tell them what we're trying to do. Then maybe they wouldn't mind keeping him a bit longer."

I didn't want to ring the stables. I was terrified in case it was Mrs Hatchet who answered. I didn't want to get chewed out again! But one of us had to ring, and I thought probably it had to be me as it was my mum who'd gone and messed up.

"OK," I said. "I'll do it."

It wasn't Mrs Hatchet; that was one relief. It was a girl I didn't know. One of the ones who helped out.

"Brave Warrior?" she said. "He's not here any more . . . he's gone."

Chapter 4

"*Gone?*" My voice came out in a terrified squawk. "You mean—"

"He's gone to some stables over Farley Down."

"Oh!"

Relief flooded through me. Just for a moment I'd really thought my legs were going to give way. My knees had turned all to jelly.

I wobbled back into the sitting-room where Mum was still wrestling with her translation.

"It's all right," I said. "You won't have to ring the sanctuary."

"Oh, Clara!" Mum stopped typing and stared at me in anguish. "They haven't —"

"No! He's gone to another stables."

"Thank heavens for that! You'd never have forgiven me."

"Well, I would," I said, "because I know you can't help forgetting things. I know your memory isn't what it was." She is always telling me this. "But I'm glad I haven't got to!"

"So am I," said Mum. "I would have felt so bad! I hate the thought of an animal being wilfully destroyed. Well, that's a very satisfactory conclusion. Now you can get down and concentrate on your homework."

You see what I mean? She is *obsessed*. And then she goes on about me and Jilly! At least we admit that animals are our passion.

"You can have this table," said Mum. "I'm about finished."

"I must just go and tell Jilly," I pleaded.

"Well, don't be on that phone for hours!"

"I won't!" I said. "I'm only going to *tell* her."

I suppose it was a bit naughty of me, really. When Jilly came on the phone I said, in these very low *sepulchral* tones, "Warrior has gone."

"G-gone?" quavered Jilly.

"To another stables!"

I expected her to give a great screech of

50

delight. Instead, in tragic tones, she cried, "But he's not supposed to work!"

I'd been so overjoyed to think that Warrior wasn't being sent to the knacker's yard that this hadn't occurred to me.

"Maybe they won't expect him to work," I said.

"So what would they want him for?"

"Just to . . . go out on beginner rides?" I said.

"He was already doing that! Everybody said he wasn't earning his keep."

"Well! I don't know," I said. "All I know is, he's not being turned into horse meat!"

And I slammed the phone down. I was just about sick of Jilly always pouring cold water over everything. Always raising objections. Always finding something to niggle about. Why couldn't she just be *happy*, for once?

I stumped grumpily off to have some tea and do my boring homework. It was maths, and I'm useless at maths. So is Mum, unfortunately. She can help me with most everything else, but she says that as far as she is concerned maths is just gobbledygook. Well! To me it's like *double* gobbledygook. I usually go wailing to Jilly, who is some kind of mathematical genius, but when you've just slammed the phone down on someone you can't very well ask them if they'll kindly do your maths homework for you.

I scrawled down lots of gobbledygook answers and spent the rest of the evening curled up on the sofa with Mud, watching television. I didn't particularly want to watch television and afterwards I wished I hadn't because they had something horrid on about people killing elephants to steal their tusks, which upset me. I went to bed feeling in total despair with the world and humankind. I also had lots of annoying little flickers of anxiety darting to and fro about my brain. Why *had* those stables taken Warrior? What did they want him for? What were they going to do with him?

I tossed and turned all night long. I felt like battering on my bedroom wall and waking Jilly. (Her bed is just the other side.) If I couldn't sleep, I didn't see why she should. It was all her fault!

Of course I apologized next morning. We are never mad at each other for long. Jilly apologized, too. She said, "I know I always look on the gloomy side. It's one of my faults."

By nature I am rather an optimist. I tend to see silver linings behind the darkest cloud! And I always, *always* say that a cup is half full. Never half empty! So it is probably just as well if one of us is a bit more cautious.

I said this to Jilly and she said, "Yes, but sometimes I am a worry guts. Warrior's probably gone to a place where they don't mind if he doesn't earn his keep."

"You mean, because they're rich?" I said.

"Well, they could be," said Jilly. "Or they could just be like us and love animals."

That cheered us both up. We had visions of Warrior living in a beautiful green meadow with lots of juicy grass and interesting plants for him to nibble at and trees to keep the sun off him, and a big cosy barn where he could go if it was cold. And there would be all the other horses, all the stable horses, to keep him company, and he would never have to work again, except maybe just the odd amble through the countryside when the weather was nice.

That is how horses *ought* to be kept. Not shut away in boxes.

I was ever so happy, thinking of Warrior in his field! It didn't bother me in the least when Mr Trimble told us to mark one another's maths homework and I got one out of ten. Jilly was more upset than me.

"I'm sorry," she whispered. "It's just all wrong!"

"Doesn't matter," I said. A person can't be good at everything.

Mr Trimble could hardly believe it!

"Clara Carter," he said, "what is the matter with you?"

Earnestly I said, "I don't think I have a mathematical type of brain."

"Oh, don't you?" said Mr Trimble. "Well, *I* don't think you pay attention!"

I assured him that I did. "But it's very difficult when you can't understand anything."

"You understand that two and two make four," said Mr Trimble. "Don't you?"

Geraldine Hooper sniggered.

"*Yes?*" said Mr Trimble. "Two and two make four?"

I nodded.

"In that case –" he waved my maths homework triumphantly in front of my face – "how do you come to the answer minus five for question number two?"

Everybody in the class just fell about. Even Jilly giggled. An answer of minus five was apparently ridiculous. How was I to know? I thought very hard of Warrior in his field.

"It's all gobbledygook," I said.

"You can say that again!" roared Mr Trimble.

Jilly told me at breaktime that she would have helped me if I'd gone round to her place, but I assured her that it was absolutely unimportant.

"So long as Warrior's safe, I don't care about anything else."

That evening when we got home from school we tried helping Benjy teach Mud to sit. We spent a whole hour at it and used up a whole bag of dog biscuits. We were ever so patient. But he still didn't sit!

It didn't mean he was stupid, any more than I was stupid not being able to do maths.

"It just means he's not a sitting sort of dog," I said.

"It might mean we're not teaching him the right way," said Jilly.

Yes! Like Mr Trimble wasn't teaching me maths the right way. I bet that was it!

On Wednesday, old No-Neck came marching up to us.

"Did you hear about Warrior?" she said.

"Yes," I said, at exactly the same moment as Jilly went "No!" It is quite true that she looks on the gloomy side. She was already preparing for meltdown!

"He's gone to another stables," I said.

"Farley Down. I wouldn't want any horse of mine going there."

"Why not?"

"They've got a foul reputation," said No-Neck. "They ride their horses into the ground."

"But Warrior can't be used! Only for beginner rides."

"They wouldn't care. They send their horses out *lame*. And they don't feed them properly. I knew a girl that used to ride there. She had to stop because she said all their horses were knackered. It'd have been better if he'd been sent for slaughter," said No-Neck. "At least it would all be over."

Well! That put paid to our happiness. We were plunged once again into deepest gloom. Except that now it was me who was the pessimist and Jilly who tried to look on the bright side.

"You know what No-Neck's like," she said. "She just says things to get at us."

"That's what we thought before," I muttered, "when she said about Warrior going to the knacker's."

"Yes, and he didn't go!"

"But now he's been sent somewhere even worse! Some horrible place that's going to work him to death!"

"We don't know that," said Jilly. "It's only something she's heard. She could even be making it up."

But I had a horrid feeling that she wasn't. When you've got your own pony and you move in horsey circles, you get to hear about these things.

"Old Hatchet wouldn't have let him go there if they weren't going to treat him properly," said Jilly.

"She might if they gave her some money," I said. "Or even if they just came and took him for free. She was going to have to *pay* the knacker people."

"Really?" Jilly looked frightened. She hadn't known that. It was something Christy had told me.

"Let's go to the stables after school," I said, "and see if we can find out."

We had to go home first, as always, to stop our mums from having panic attacks. (SCHOOLGIRLS KNOCKED OFF BIKES BY HIT AND RUN DRIVER! SCHOOL-GIRLS GONE MISSING! SCHOOLGIRLS ABDUCTED! They could write a book about the things they imagine happening to us.)

"We're going to the stables," I told Mum. "We'll take Mud with us."

"Why the stables?" Mum wanted to know. "Why not just over the fields?"

Any minute now she was going to start on about homework.

"The stables are a good half-hour away. By the time you've been there and back—"

"We'll run!" I said.

"But Mud doesn't need that long a walk! He's already been out with Mr Hennessy. Why d—"

"Mum, we've got to!" I yelled. "It's important!"

I wasn't going to tell her why. She'd only groan. And maybe it might just turn out to be a false alarm. Oh, I did hope so!

We found Christy at the stables. She said, "Hi, you two! Good news about Warrior. Did you hear?"

Jilly and me looked at each other and grinned. Christy though it was good news! So much for No-Neck.

All the same, now that we were here I thought we ought to make certain.

"They won't work him to death," I said, "will they?"

"They shouldn't be working him at all! They know he's got damaged lungs."

"Just beginner rides," I said.

"Yes, and maybe a bit of ring work."

"Are they rich?" said Jilly.

Christy looked bewildered. "Rich?"

"Or just animal lovers," I said.

"Oh! I see what you mean. I don't know; why?"

"Someone told us they rode their horses into the ground," I mumbled.

Christy frowned. "I'm sure Pippa wouldn't have let him go there if she hadn't thought they were going to look after him."

There was a silence.

"Who told you, anyway?" said Christy.

"No-N— I mean, Puffin," I said.

"Oh! Well! Puffin. She's a bit of a doom merchant. I shouldn't worry about it, if I were you. At least he didn't go for horse meat."

Jilly and I stayed silent.

"See you at the weekend?" said Christy. "Saturday? Sunday?"

Jilly opened her mouth. She was going to say yes. But I stepped in very smartly and said, "Unfortunately we can't make it this week."

Jilly looked at me in surprise.

"Why can't we?" she hissed, as we left the stables.

" 'Cos I had a sudden thought . . . I think we ought to go to Farley Down and ride."

"Farley Down? No-Neck said all their horses are knackered!"

Jilly may be a mathematical genius but there are times when she is *really* slow on the uptake.

"I want to check on Warrior," I said. "I want to see him for myself! We need to make sure he's all right."

Jilly heaved a sigh. "Christy doesn't really know, does she?"

Christy hadn't lived here that long; not long enough to be up on all the horsey gossip. No-Neck had lived here all her life. *And* she had been riding since she was tiny.

"I'm going to ring and book," I said.

"Tell them I want something gentle!" pleaded Jilly. "Not a race horse!"

Jilly needn't have worried: there weren't any race horses at Farley Down. It was a mean, miserable sort of place. No-Neck hadn't been making up stories. I hated it the minute I saw it! All the buildings were falling to pieces. The yard was covered in hay and horse dung and bits of machinery. And all the poor horses were kept in tiny stalls, so narrow they could hardly turn round. They couldn't have turned round anyway, because they were tethered with their heads facing the far end so they had nothing to stare at but a bare blank wall.

It is *cruel* to keep horses tied up like that.

The man who owned the place was little and scrawny and walked with a limp. He was so bow-legged you could have kicked a football through his legs. He looked as if maybe he had been a jockey. His name was Chislett, and I just bet that's what he did to people. Chiselled them.

We looked all round but we couldn't see Warrior anywhere, though lots of the stalls were empty.

Two tatty-looking ponies were brought out for me and Jilly. They were called Dusty and Solo and they were ever such a pathetic pair. I felt so sorry for them! They made Jet and Cherokee seem like quality (which we knew they weren't because No-Neck had taken care to tell us).

The girl who took us out was called Natalie. She was old Chisel's daughter. She didn't look much like her dad as she was quite long and skinny, but she was sullen like him. She hardly talked at all. And the ride was dead boring! Those poor ponies didn't even want to trot, let alone canter. And I think they'd forgotten what it felt like to enjoy a good gallop. Jilly was probably quite relieved, but I began to understand how No-Neck had felt that first day, when Christy wouldn't let her take off.

I pushed and poked and prodded until Dusty broke into a reluctant trot and I was able to catch up with Natalie.

"Have you got a horse called Brave Warrior?" I said.

"Dunno," said Natalie. "Might have."

"He's big and beautiful and black, with a white blaze," I said.

"Oh, yeah. Just got him. He's out on a hack."

Cold hands clutched at my heart.

"But he's got damaged lungs!" I said.

"Yeah?"

"He was in a fire! He's only fit for beginner rides!"

"Who says?"

"It's true! Honestly!"

Natalie turned, and looked me up and down.

"What are you? Some kind of expert?"

I felt like telling her I was an official Animal Lover, but I guessed she would only sneer.

"My dad's been around horses all his life," she said. "He knows what he's doing."

I swallowed. "Why does he keep them all tied up?"

"Makes it easier to muck out."

"But don't they get bored? They've got nothing to look at! And they can't talk to each other."

"They get enough to do," said Natalie.

She was one of those people it is impossible to have a proper conversation with. I grew more and more depressed and more and more worried about Brave Warrior. I fell back and waited for Jilly, who couldn't make Solo move any faster than a slow walk.

"This is hateful!" she said.

"I know. I think No-Neck was right."

"Did you ask about Warrior?"

"He's out on a hack."

"Out on a *hack*?"

I nodded, and my hat almost fell off. All the hats at Farley Down were either too big or too small. Christy wouldn't have let us go out wearing hats that didn't fit, but at Farley Down they didn't seem to care.

"What are we going to do?" whispered Jilly.

"I don't know," I said. "But we've got to do something!"

The nightmare ride came to an end at last. We clopped back into the filthy stableyard and Natalie took the ponies and led them away. We were about to go to the office and pay – I was trying to screw up my courage to say something to old Chisel – when there was a clattering of hooves and we saw the hack returning. They were cantering, flat out, down the lane. Among them was Warrior.

Our poor Warrior! A huge great brute of a red-faced man was sitting on his back. He looked like a heavyweight wrestler.

They pulled up in the yard. All the other horses snorted and tossed their heads, but not Warrior. I have never seen a poor horse look so dejected. He stood there, drooping, the picture of horsey misery. His head was down, his flanks were heaving. He was covered in sweat.

Before I even had time to stop and think about it, I had gone rushing forward.

"That horse has damaged lungs!" I shouted. "He shouldn't be ridden like that!"

Chapter 5

A silence fell over the yard. Everyone was looking at me. The big, fat, red-faced man slowly dismounted, and oh! I was so relieved. At least it meant poor Warrior could breathe a bit easier.

I stroked his neck, all flecked with white foam, while the other riders just sat there, gaping. The poor boy was trembling, his ears pulled right back. A sure sign of horsey distress.

The big fat man said, "We'll see about this," and went stamping off across the yard.

"Oh, Warrior!" I whispered. I kissed his soft velvety nose and he did his best to nuzzle me. Then I put my finger in his mouth and wobbled his lower lip for him, but he didn't push his head against me or flicker his ears as he used to. He was too tired, and too unhappy

Natalie had appeared. She yanked Warrior's bridle away from me. Then she gave me this absolutely filthy look and said, "You'd do better to mind your own business."

"But look at him!" I cried. "He shouldn't be ridden like that!"

"What's it to you?" she said. "What do you know about anything?"

I opened my mouth to say that I was an Animal Lover and had sworn to fight for animals, but before I could get any further than "I'm an an—" there was the sound of shouting and old Chisel roared into the yard. He had a rake in his hand and he was making straight for me.

"What the devil is going on?" he bawled. "Who the hell do you think you are, poxy well coming here, laying down the law? Whose poxy horse is it?"

I nearly put ***** instead of all the swear words. Instead, I've just changed them slightly, so they're not so bad. I mean, don't get me wrong. I don't mind the odd bit of swearing, I do

68

quite a lot of it myself as a matter of fact. Like when Mud goes and stamps all over my homework or jumps into my bed with dirty feet, I yell things like "Look what you've done, you great palooka!"

Another thing I sometimes say is "Hot damn!"

Mum tells me off for it, but I think it is simply a way of relieving one's feelings. But I don't go round saying the things that old Chisel said!

All the other people had got off their horses and were kind of looking the other way, like they didn't want to be a part of it. Jilly was waiting at the entrance to the yard, nervously peering in and praying – I bet! – that she didn't have to come to my rescue.

I was praying she didn't have to come to my rescue, too. I was really scared, the way old Chisel was waving that rake around. His eyes had gone all bulgy, as if they were about to come bursting out of their sockets, and I could see a vein in his neck going throb, throb, throb.

I suppose if I am to be honest I would have to admit that what I really felt like doing was jumping on my bike and cycling away just as fast as I could. It was only the sight of poor dejected Warrior, standing there with his head hanging down, that gave me courage.

"Look at him!" I pleaded. "He's not well!"

Old Chisel turned and jabbed the rake at Natalie.

"Get that poxy horse back in its box! And you –" he prodded at me – "get out of my yard! If you ever come here again, spreading lies about my stock, I'll have your guts for garters! I'll have you up for libel!"

The red-faced man was hovering, trying to get a word in.

"Jeff, Jeff!"

"What's your problem?" snarled old Chisel.

"I just wanted to know . . . about the horse. Is it true?"

"Of course it's not poxy well true! What do you think? I send my customers out on poxy knackered horses? You take her poxy word before mine?"

"No. No!" Red Face backed away. "I just wanted to make sure."

"Well! Now you have."

"Yes." Red Face flapped a hand. "I'll – ah – see you next week."

Red Face disappeared. All the other riders had disappeared. It was just me and old Chisel – and Jilly still quivering at the entrance.

"He really has got damaged lungs," I whispered.

"So? What do you want me to do? Send him for horse meat?"

"Just treat him *gently*," I begged.

"Listen, you poxy little pip squeak! These are animals. They are here to be ridden. And as long as they are capable of being ridden, they will be ridden. End of story. Right? You got that? Do I make myself clear? Now, hoppit!"

"*Please*," I said.

He swung round. "Are you thick, or something? Didn't you hear what I just said?"

"Yes, but I'm an official Animal Lover," I said. "I've sworn to protect animals. I can't just walk away and forget about it!"

"No?" He stuck his face close to mine. "So what are you planning to do?"

I could have said that I was going to report him

to the RSPCA, but somehow I didn't think it would bother him too much. He looked like the sort of man who is always being reported and always gets away with it.

"If we found a s-sanctuary," I stammered, "would you l-let him g-go?"

"Well, now! That would all depend."

"On wh-what?" I said. I didn't like the expression that had come slithering into his eyes. All crafty and grasping. It made him seem even nastier than when he was shouting four-letter words.

"On how much you'd be prepared to give me."

"G-*give* you?" I said.

"Well, you didn't think I'd let him go for nothing, did you? I paid good money for that horse!"

"H-how much?" I said.

"Well . . . let's see." He rubbed a hand over his sandpapery chin. "I reckon he's still got a few weeks' work left in him. So it's not just a question of how much I paid, but how much I could make."

"*How much?*" I was almost jigging up and down with frustration.

"Say three hundred quid and he's yours."

Three hundred! My dismay must have shown in my face.

"Take it or leave it. But don't set foot in my stable again spreading vicious lies amongst my customers or you'll be in trouble. *Dead* trouble. I mean it!"

I went tottering off to join Jilly.

"Three hundred pounds!" I moaned. "We can never make three hundred pounds!"

"We could make some of it," said Jilly.

"What good's some of it! Some's not enough! He said three hundred!"

"We could pay by instalment."

"Oh!" I gaped at her. Jilly is really *brilliant* when it comes to finance. "D'you think he'd let us?"

"Only one way to find out," said Jilly.

"You mean—"

"Go back and ask him."

"What, m-me?" I said.

"Well . . . one of us."

There was a pause.

"I'll do it," said Jilly. She made her hands into two tight fists, like a boxer. "You wait there!"

73

"Be careful," I begged, "he's violent!"

By way of reply, Jilly just made the sort of gesture that some of the boys in our class make when they want to shock you. Not that they shock me! I am unshockable. But I was quite surprised at Jilly! Being an Animal Lover has made her quite ferocious. When I first met her she was ever so timid. I was the one who always went rushing in. Jilly was the one who did all the thinking and came up with all the good arguments. These days, she goes rushing in, as well!

And I try to do a bit more thinking. That is only fair.

Now it was me standing at the entrance, quivering. I couldn't help wondering what I would do if old Chisel really did turn violent. Should I go rushing to the rescue, or would it be better to jump on my bike and madly pedal off to get help? Our mums would be furious! They tell us over and over "Not to get mixed up in anything dangerous". But you can't always help it. You can't just walk away from things.

I jiggled about from one foot to the other, wishing that Jilly would come back out.

From where I was, I could see across the horrid littered yard to the box where Warrior had been taken. I could see Natalie still in there with him. She seemed to be rubbing him down, and I was relieved about that. I remembered Christy telling us that it was bad to let a horse stay covered in sweat. All the same, I hated the thought of having to go away and leave him in the hands of such hateful people. Our gentle giant! He must be so confused and so frightened. He deserved better than this!

Jilly still hadn't come back out. I was just beginning to think that I would have to pluck up the courage to go and see what was happening, when thank goodness she reappeared. She didn't look as if old Chisel had attacked her. At any rate, she wasn't covered in blood.

"Are you all right?" I said.

She nodded, so that all her blond bubbly curls bounced up and down.

"Yes! He said if we managed to find half, he'd let us have Warrior and we could pay off the rest on hire purchase . . . a bit every week."

"Oh! That's brilliant," I said.

I would never have thought of that. Now all we had to do was find a hundred and fifty pounds . . . *urgently*. We couldn't bear the thought of that poor frightened horse having to stay there a minute longer than necessary.

We discussed all the ways we could think of to make money.

Jilly said that she had some in her account at the building society. "But Mum won't let me touch it!"

I said that I didn't have any at all.

"We could always use our riding money," said Jilly.

"What, without telling them?"

"Well. . ." Jilly shrugged. She looked a bit uncomfortable; we don't usually deceive our mums.

"I *hate* the thought of giving money to that loathsome man," I said.

"So do I," said Jilly.

But sometimes you just have to grit your teeth. After all, it was to save a horse's life. A poor, innocent, ill-used horse who had never hurt anyone but had just done his best to please.

I reminded Jilly of this, and she said that I was quite right and we must think of Warrior and not worry about the money.

"Except," I said, "where to get it from."

"Well, if we use next week's riding money, that's thirty pounds before we start. Then there's our pocket money; that makes forty. Then if our mums would let us have a week's pocket money in *advance*, that would make fifty . . . that would only leave a hundred!"

"*Only*," I said.

"Don't be such a glump! I'm the one that's supposed to look on the black side."

"It's just that I've never even *had* a hundred pounds," I said.

"Me neither," said Jilly. "Except in the building society, where I can't get hold of it. But it can't be that difficult!"

"Maybe we could sell things?"

"Yes! We could sell things! That's a good idea!"

"Let's go home and find something!"

We cycled home as fast as our pedals would take us.

"Meet you in half an hour," I said.

The minute I got indoors I was ambushed by Benjy and Mud.

"Clawa, Clawa!" cried Benjy. "I dord Dubba die dowd!"

"You've taught Mud to lie down? That's clever," I said.

He wanted to show me, but I said a bit impatiently that I had things to do. I set off up the stairs.

"Clara!"

Bother. That was Mum. She sounded . . . not pleased.

"Mum, I've got things to do!" I yelled.

"Could you come in here for a minute first, please?"

I pulled a face. Sometimes a person just cannot call their life their own.

"What is it?"

"What do you mean, what is it? Don't take that tone of voice with me!" said Mum. "I thought we'd made a bargain? In return for your pocket money you would dust and vacuum your room *and put your things away* every Saturday morning?"

"Oh. Well! Yes. I was going to."

"When?" said Mum. "It is now Saturday afternoon!"

"I'll do it later. I will, I promise! Oh, and Mum –" I turned back, putting on my sweetest smile – "Do you think you could let me have two weeks' pocket money in advance?"

"No," said Mum. "Why?"

"Well . . . um. I need it," I said. I didn't want to tell her it was for Warrior. I knew she would only start on again about me being obsessed.

"What do you need it *for*?"

"Just things."

"What things?"

I groaned inside my head.

"I just want to buy something," I said. "A horsey thing."

Well, it was sort of true. I mean, if a horse isn't a horsey thing, what is?

"It's going cheap," I said. "It's only on offer for a short while."

And that probably *was* true. Alas! I just couldn't see our poor darling Warrior lasting for much longer, the way he was being treated.

"Mum, *please*!" I said. "It's *desperate*!"

"I'll think about it," said Mum. "When you've cleaned your room."

I flew upstairs, with Mud and Benjy hot on my heels. Benjy wanted to know what was going on. He seemed to think it was some kind of a game. So did Mud. He thinks everything's a game!

I said, "Benjy, this is something *very serious*. Jilly and me are trying to make some money so that we can rescue a poor sick horse. We're looking for things we can sell. But you mustn't tell Mum!"

Benjy promised solemnly that he wouldn't. He said that he had some things I could sell and he went off to look for them, taking Mud along with him. For which I was grateful! Mud is such a bright dog, he always wants to be part of everything. He does his best to help, but when he tramples on things and overturns things and worst of all, starts *eating* things, it is really more of a hindrance.

My little store of belongings is pathetically small. I whizzed through them in about ten minutes, trying to find anything that I could do without and that Mum wouldn't miss. It wasn't any use taking clothes, even ones I hated. She'd be bound to notice they'd gone. It would be, "Whatever happened to that nice little blue jacket?" or "Where did that sweet little cardigan go that Nan knitted for you?" And then she'd accuse me of leaving them somewhere. "You're so careless, Clara! Do you think we're made of money?"

In the end, all I could come up with were a few books (ones that I'd grown out of), some china ornaments that I really hated to part with (I had to keep reminding myself that Warrior was more important), a bar of soap in the shape of a cow that I'd never been able to bring myself to use, and a few bits and pieces, such as jigsaw puzzles and painting sets and stuff that had been at the back of my cupboard for so long I thought Mum was sure to have forgotten about it.

I had just fetched a big plastic carrier bag from the kitchen and packed everything into it when Benjy staggered in carrying what looked like his entire wardrobe. T-shirts, sweatshirts, shorts, jeans. Even shoes and socks! He dumped it all on my bed, informing me proudly that it was for "the poor sick horse". I didn't know what to say! I didn't want to hurt his feelings but I had to explain that Mum would go demented if I sold all his clothes.

We took them back to his room and he let me help myself to a few books and toys, instead. He was ever so anxious to help the poor sick horse! I really think that one day, when he is old enough, he will become an Animal Lover himself.

Jilly was waiting for me, with a big plastic bag of her own. She had had the same problem as I had, trying to find stuff that her mum wouldn't miss.

"I didn't like to ask her," she said. "She told me the other day that I was taking this whole animal thing too far."

"Yes, mine says that," I agreed.

"But how *can* you take it too far?" said Jilly. "Most people don't take it far enough!"

"Most people don't take it anywhere at all," I said.

We staggered into the village with our carrier bags and headed for the indoor market that is held every Saturday. What we thought we'd do, we'd go round all the stalls and ask the stall holders if they were interested. We would see who offered us the best price.

"I mean, *look*," said Jilly, opening her bag to show me. "A padded coat hanger!"

"What's a padded coat hanger?"

"It's a coat hanger that's padded . . . it's even got a little bag of smelly stuff hanging off it."

"Way out!" I said.

"People like them," insisted Jilly. "Someone gave it to my mum and she gave it to me 'cos she didn't want it. And look, here's a bottle of perfume! Mum opened it just to have a sniff. It's called *Mysteries of the Orient*. I should think anyone would want that!"

"And my china ornaments," I said.

Well! You would have thought so. I don't know what is wrong with people. Those were *good* ornaments. There was a little squirrel eating a nut and a little donkey pulling a cart and the dearest, cutest little rabbit wearing a red suit. I know the donkey had a chip out of one of his ears, but it hardly showed. Yet all we got, for the books and the ornaments, and the padded coat hanger, and all the other lovely things we'd lugged down the street, was a measly five pounds! I would have thought we'd get *at least* twenty.

Jilly was a bit despondent about it, as well.

"Still, five pounds is five pounds," she said.

"But we'll never get enough at this rate!" I wailed. "I haven't got anything else I can sell!"

"No." Jilly stamped viciously on an empty Coke tin and scrunched it flat. "There've got to be other ways of making money!"

We agreed that we would meet up next day and discuss it. Then we would write out a list: **WAYS OF MAKING MONEY.**

"And then," said Jilly, "we'll try them all, one after another, until we get enough!"

Chapter 6

In the end, I had to tell Mum why it was I wanted my pocket money in advance. She said that a vague "horsey thing" wasn't good enough.

"Be more specific!"

I said, *"Why?* Why do I have to?" I could hear my voice all whiny and protesting.

Mum said, "I want to be sure you're not throwing it away on something stupid."

I felt like shouting, "It's my money! I can spend it how I like!" But then I thought she might start on again about my room not being cleaned and all my clothes lying about, so I muttered, "It's Warrior."

"Oh, not again!" cried Mum. "I thought that was all settled?"

"Well, it's not. They're not looking after him

properly. Mum, they're *killing* him! They just don't care! And he's all tied up in a horrid little box where he can't turn round, it's like a prison cell!"

"Maybe horses don't mind being tied up," said Mum.

"They do! They hate it! It's not right! They ought to be free to run about. You shouldn't *ever* keep a horse tied up so it can't move. It's wicked! It's—"

"All right, all right!" Mum held up her hands. "I give in! You don't have to lecture me. What exactly do you plan to do with this money you're asking me for?"

I brightened. "We're going to buy him back!"

"With two weeks' pocket money?"

"Well – no. We'll need a bit more than that."

"A good bit more, I should think!"

"We're going to discuss it, this morning."

"*After* you've done your homework."

"Oh, well, yes! Of course," I said, trying to sound keen and eager. "Of course we'll do our homework *first*."

"Hmm!" said Mum.

"I suppose *you* don't have any ideas how to make money?" I said.

Mum gave a hollow laugh.

"No, Mum, this is serious!" I said.

Mum said, "Oh, Clara, making money is always serious. I spend my entire life struggling to make money! I really don't know what to suggest. Why don't you try asking Meg?"

That was what it always came back to: ask Meg. Well, this time we weren't going to! We'd bothered her quite enough. This was something we had to do *by ourselves*. And anyway, as Jilly reminded me, Meg was away trying to raise money for her own animals.

"She's doing this walk thingy."

"A sponsored walk!" I looked at Jilly, excited. "Maybe that's what we could do?"

"*Us?* Where would we walk?"

"Anywhere! Round the playing field."

"But who'd sponsor us?"

"Your mum – my mum – Mr Hennessy. People at school. Anybody! What you have to do is," I said, "you have to print some forms and get people to put their names down saying how much they'll sponsor you for."

"How do we get to print forms?"

It is simply no use losing your cool when Jilly is in one of these moods. You just have to be patient.

"We'll do them on Mum's computer," I said. "*I'll* do them. Then we'll get people to fill them in and then all we have to do is just walk. Write it down! Make a list."

Obediently, Jilly picked up her pen and wrote, **WAYS TO MAKE MONEY** on a page torn from my homework book. **No. 1. Sponsered walk**.

"Actually it's spelt with an O," I said. "Not that it matters."

"Then why mention it?" snapped Jilly.

"I just thought you'd like to know," I said. "You don't have to bite my head off."

Jilly muttered something about people who could add two and two together and make them come to five. I haven't the *faintest* idea what she was talking about.

"Think of something else!" I said.

We sat and thought. Jilly chewed her pen, I

chewed my thumb nail. Every now and again Jilly would go, "We could always—" And I would go, "What?" And Jilly would go, "No. That's no use!"

If it wasn't Jilly, it was me.

"How about—"

"What?"

"No! That wouldn't work."

"We've got to think of *something*!" cried Jilly.

"I know!" I sprang up. A brilliant idea had come to me. "If we cycled out to Tesco's we could make a fortune taking people's trolleys back for them!"

"What, now?" said Jilly.

"Why not?"

"On a *Sunday*?"

"It's what people do on a Sunday. They go to Tesco's. And there's the DIY, as well. We could make *oodles*!"

Jilly still seemed a bit hesitant, but as she couldn't think of anything better she agreed that we should at least try it.

I said to Mum, "We're cycling out to Tesco's to get the pounds on people's shopping trolleys."

"Well, just be polite about it," said Mum. "Some people might not want you to get the pounds on their trolleys."

"In which case, we *wouldn't*," I said.

What did she think? We were going to start mugging old ladies?

Tesco's was simply swarming, just as I'd known it would be. So was the DIY. Jilly and me chained our bikes to some railings and set off towards the trolley park. Then suddenly, at the last minute, Jilly got cold feet.

"I don't think I can do this," she whispered.

"But there's nothing to it!" I said. "You just go up and ask people."

"But I don't know what to say!"

"Look, I'll show you. It's easy!"

I marched up to two women that were standing talking. One of them had a full trolley: she was obviously going back to her car. The other had an empty trolley: she had obviously just *come* from her car.

"Excuse me," I said, ever so polite. "Would you like me to take your trolley back for you?"

"Oh, yes? And then what happens?" said the woman. "I never see you again!"

"Well," I said, "you would probably *see* me, because I'm going to be here all afternoon."

"But I wouldn't see my pound," she said, "would I?"

And she twitched the trolley away from me as if she thought I was some kind of a thief. As I went back to Jilly I heard her grumbling, "These kids! Think they can get away with murder."

"What happened?" said Jilly.

"Oh, she was just a dweeb. I'll try another one. Watch this!"

This time I went up to an old lady who I could see had trouble walking.

"Excuse me, may I take your trolley?" I said.

That old lady! She got hold of *quite* the wrong end of the stick.

"You give me a pound," she said, "and it's yours."

I knew that Jilly was watching me. I couldn't flunk out a second time!

"Really, I meant could I take it and keep the pound," I gabbled. "It's not for me, it's for a poor sick horse I'm trying to rescue. I'm an Animal Lover, you see." And I jabbed a finger at the badge I always wear.

Actually, that old lady turned out to be ace. She said that she couldn't afford to let me have the whole pound but if I took the trolley back and saved her legs she'd give me 20p.

"For the animals."

Well, I mean, it was better than nothing.

After that, I told everyone what I was collecting for. Some people were sympathetic, but lots couldn't have cared less. And a few were really horrible. Jilly came up to me in tears because one woman had been extra specially mean.

"She said she had a good mind to call the police!"

"Well, she can't call the police 'cos we're not doing anything wrong," I said. "It's a free country! We're just trying to earn a bit of money."

Jilly scrubbed at her eyes. "How long have we got to go on?"

Poor old Jilly! She hates having to go up to complete strangers and talk to them. I don't mind; I'll talk to anyone. The nastier some people were, the more determined I became. I reminded Jilly that it was for Warrior. I said, "Think of that poor frightened horse shut up in his prison cell . . . we've *got* to get enough money to rescue him!"

We stayed in the trolley park until closing time and then we thought we had better go home before our mums started on their panic attacks. (SCHOOLGIRLS ABDUCTED IN TESCO TROLLEY PARK. . .) In any case, I didn't want Jilly reduced to a nervous wreck! We still had our sponsored walk to do.

"How much have we made?" said Jilly.

We turned out our pockets. Jilly had made six pounds and a French franc that someone had given her. I had made £10.20. Jilly promised that she would draw up proper accounts as soon as she'd had her tea.

"We have to keep a note of how much we've earned."

When we got home, Mum asked me how we'd done. Proudly I announced that we had made £16.20 and a French franc.

"Oh, dear!" said Mum. "That's not a very good return for all your hard work."

Wasn't it? I thought we'd done quite well! I said, "It's £16.20 that we didn't have before."

"I suppose that is one way of looking at it," said Mum. "Here!" She took out her purse. "Let me at least make it up to seventeen for you."

I hesitated.

"What's the matter?" said Mum. "Not accepting charity?"

"We'll accept *anything*," I said. "But I wanted you to sponsor us for our sponsored walk!"

I told Mum what we were planning and she laughed and said she thought she could probably afford to sponsor us *and* make up our hard-earned money to seventeen pounds. She was in a really good mood! (This was because she had finished her rush-job translation.) She even helped me work out the words to put on our sponsor form.

This is what the form looked like:

CLARA and JILLY are going on a SPONSORED WALK to raise money for a POOR SICK HORSE. Please help!		
Name	Signature	Amount per lap (around the sports field)

Mum filled in her name and wrote "50p" in the last column, and I then took the form next door for Jilly's mum.

"How many laps do you think you'll do?" she said.

"Oh, dozens!" said Jilly.

Jilly had become quite cheerful since having her tea and making up the accounts. Jilly's mum used to be a bookkeeping person, so Jilly knows all about that sort of thing. She'd written it all out in her tiny neat handwriting. (Mine is large and *sprawls*.)

FUND TO RESCUE WARRIOR

Amount needed	£150·00
Amount collected:	
Riding money	£30·00
Pocket money (Jilly's)	£10·00
Pocket money (Clara's)	£10·00
Sale of goods	£5·00
Trolley money	£16·20
total	£71·20
Amount still needed	£78·80

"And Mum just gave me 80p," I said, so Jilly promptly added that to the list as well.

"Now we only need seventy-eight pounds . . . but just remember, these accounts are *confidential*," she hissed.

The reason they were confidential was that our mums didn't know what we were planning to do with next Saturday's riding money! I felt a weeny bit guilty about this, especially as Mum was being so nice, but I only had to think of poor Warrior, with his heaving flanks and his head hanging down, to know that what we were doing was right.

Next morning, we took our sponsor forms into school and went round everyone in our class asking if they would sponsor us. Almost everybody did! There were just one or two people, such as for instance George Handley and his friend Roger Bone. George told me to go stick my head in a bucket of snot. Roger told me to go and eat cow dung. But this is the sort of thing they are always telling people to do. It didn't bother me.

Our sworn enemies, Geraldine and No-Neck, also didn't sign. At least, not at first. They started off on their "Why do you only care about animals?" routine. We didn't take any notice of them. Then Jilly, very bold, went up to Mr O'Shea and asked him if he would sponsor us, and oh, bliss! He put his name down for a whole pound! A pound for every lap we completed. Most people had put 10p or even just five.

We pinned the completed forms on the notice board so that everyone could see, and of course old Geraldine and No-Neck just goggled when they saw Mr O'Shea's name there!

They came up to us, later.

"We have decided," said Geraldine.

"We have come to a decision," said No-Neck.

"We will sponsor you *just this once*."

"But only for 5p because of giving everything else to Oxfam."

"For the starving children."

Jilly, in lordly fashion, thanked them for their generosity and said that every little helped.

"*However* measly."

Geraldine tossed her head and said, "So when

are you doing this walk, anyway?"

"Tomorrow," I said. "In the lunch break."

"How do we know that it's genuine?"

When Geraldine said this, everybody groaned. Someone said, "Of course it's genuine! They're Animal Lovers."

"I just wanted to make sure," said Geraldine. "That's all."

"Yes, and who's going to check on you?" said No-Neck. "There's got to be someone to check on you!"

"We'll tell you," I said, "as soon as we've done it."

"What? Walked round the field?"

"No! Rescued Warrior."

"I didn't mean that! *Dummy*. I meant who's going to check the number of laps you do?"

Oh! We hadn't thought of that. But Mercy Humphries and Darren Bickerstaff said that they would do it, so that was all right.

"I mean, I'd trust you, personally speaking," said Darren. "Some people just have suspicious minds."

"Well, but it ought to be official," said Jilly.

"That's why I'm keeping accounts."

On the way home after school we knocked on Mr Hennessy's door.

"I suppose you wouldn't sponsor us?" said Jilly.

"Oh, I expect I might," said Mr Hennessy. "What's it for? Rescuing three-toed sloths from barbarian hordes?"

We told him it was for Warrior and he wished us luck and put his name down for a pound, like Mr O'Shea. Jilly and I really began to feel that our goal was in sight.

We discussed whether to call on Mrs Cherry, who lives in the cottage next to Mr Hennessy, but as she is extremely old and easily confused, we decided not to.

"We should have enough," said Jilly, confidently. "We're getting there!"

On Tuesday, as soon as the lunch bell sounded, we rushed to the playing field to begin our walk. Darren and Mercy sat solemnly side by side on a bench, with pencils and paper, to record the number of laps.

I'd never realized quite how huge that playing field was until we started walking round it! The first lap took *twelve minutes*.

"We've got to go faster than this!" I said.

So then we speeded up and did the next lap in only nine.

"That's better!" I panted.

Round and round the playing field we pounded. Lots of people, by now, had come to watch and cheer us on. We didn't dare break into a run for fear some horrible person such as No-Neck would accuse us of cheating – "It was meant to be a sponsored *walk*!"

"Bell's going in seven minutes," warned Darren, as we completed our fifth lap.

We knew we had to do that last lap *really* fast.

"Think of Warrior, think of Warrior, think of Warrior!"

The words hammered through my brain as my feet hammered round the playing field. Left right, left right, think of Warrior, think of Warrior! Jilly told me afterwards that she had been thinking exactly the same thing.

"Bell!" shrieked Geraldine.

But we had made it! Six laps! Now all we had to do was collect the money. . .

Most people were really good, they came up to us in the afternoon break and handed over what they had promised us. Just a few said they'd forgotten and would bring it in next day, but we still staggered home with a huge pile. We'd put it all in Jilly's school bag. It weighed a tonne!

After tea, we counted it. It came to £54.14!

"And another £9.60 still to come," gloated Jilly.

She snatched up the accounts and began writing, busily.

Amount still needed   £78.00

Sponsered walk   £54-14

To come   9·60

        total   £63.74
                             ———————

Amount still needed   £14.26
                               ———————

"Look!"

"We're nearly there!"

Nearly, but not quite.

How were we going to get that last fourteen pounds?

Chapter 7

Next day at school we collected the rest of the money that people owed us. Every single person paid up! Even Geraldine and No-Neck.

But No-Neck told us something that made us really angry. She told us that old Chisel hadn't had to pay a single penny for taking Warrior!

"He didn't pay *anything*. Mrs Hart let him have him for free. I told her you were collecting money to buy him back and she said you were crazy. He's just conning you."

Well! Jilly and I were pretty furious, as you can image. Old Chisel had told us outright lies.

It takes a lot to make Jilly angry – I mean, real hopping mad kind of angry – but I could see that she was truly incensed. She wanted to go racing out of school right there and then to tell old Chisel what she thought of him.

"He's nothing but a rotten slimy cheat!"

I said, "He's worse than a cheat, he's a horse murderer."

"So's Hatchet Face! She must have known what sort of person he was!"

"Course she did. They're horsey people. They all know each other."

"He can't get away with this!" panted Jilly.

She was striding up and down the playground, practically frothing at the mouth. I don't think I've ever seen her quite so worked up.

"The awful thing is," I said glumly, "he probably can."

Warrior was his horse. He could ask whatever he liked for him.

"If we go and yell at him, he might decide we can't have him at all. The *priority*," I said, "is to rescue Warrior."

Once Jilly had calmed down a bit, she could see that I was right. We had to get that hundred and fifty pounds! As soon as Warrior was safe, she could go and yell at old Chisel as much as she wanted.

"I will!" said Jilly. "Don't you worry! I shall tell him I'm going to report him. I shall tell the newspapers. I shall tell everyone not to ride there. I shall—"

"Burst a blood vessel, if you're not careful." That was No-Neck, strolling past with Geraldine.

"What does she think she knows about horses anyway?" said Geraldine. "She's only a beginner."

I tugged Jilly away before she could get into a slanging match. We had more important things to think about! Such as, where the last fourteen pounds was going to come from.

"It's no use me asking Mum for more pocket money," I said. "I just know she won't give it to me."

"Neither will mine," said Jilly. "And she *won't* let me have my building society money. I've begged and begged her, but she says it's for when I'm twenty-one. What good's that? I need it *now*!"

"They just don't understand."

We racked our brains all the rest of the day. We racked them through French and history and PSE, and double beastly maths and even netball, and still nothing came.

"*Money!*" cried Jilly, as we changed after netball. "How do we get *money*?"

Someone said, "Do a bank job!" and everyone giggled.

"Seriously," I said.

"You could hold a raffle," said Mercy Humphries.

"How?"

"'S easy! You just get some prizes and buy some tickets and sell them at 50p each and then pick the winning numbers out of a hat."

"But how do you make *money*?"

"Well, mostly the prizes get given for nothing, so you get to keep all the 50ps. You can make hundreds."

It seemed too good to be true!

It was. A rather know-it-all girl called Alice Ray busy-bodily informed us that you couldn't hold raffles just like that.

"You have to have permission. Otherwise it's illegal."

"Who says?" said Jilly.

"It just is. It's against the law. As a matter of

fact," said Alice, "what you did yesterday was probably against the law, too."

"What, walking round the playing field?"

"Getting people to give you money. My dad says it shouldn't have been allowed."

We stared at her in dismay.

"He's not going to make us give it back?" wailed Jilly.

"No, because I told him it was for a horse and that you're Animal Lovers and it's your mission in life. But you'd better not try holding a raffle. You could get done for it."

It was horribly dispiriting. Jilly and me discussed it as we cycled home.

"You just can't do *anything*!" said Jilly.

"I thought it was supposed to be a free country," I grumbled.

"That's what they *tell* you."

"So why is it every time you just lift a finger to try and save a poor ill-treated animal they threaten to do you?"

"Obviously because it's *not* a free country," fumed Jilly. "It's all full of stupid rules and regulations."

"It's a pity the rules and regulations don't stop them torturing animals!"

Mr Hennessy was getting out of his car as we turned into Honeypot Lane.

"Hallo!" he said. "How's the fighting fund?"

"Pardon?" said Jilly.

"The fund-raising! How's it going?"

Well! We didn't need a second invitation. We immediately skidded to a halt and poured out all our grievances, one after another. Old Chisel and old Hatchet and Alice Ray's dad and everything you tried to do being against the law unless it was torturing animals which nobody except Jilly and me seemed to care about.

"Not even our mums! They just groan and go, oh, not *again*!"

"Mine won't even let me have my own money that was given to me by my gran!"

"*Everybody* is against us," I said.

"I know the feeling! It's a bit of a pig's ear, isn't it?" said Mr Hennessy. "How much have you managed to collect?"

"One hundred and thirty-five pounds and seventy-four p," said Jilly.

I don't know how she remembers these things! If it's not a round number, it just goes right out of my head.

"That sounds pretty good to me," said Mr Hennessy. "I'll tell you what! Would you like to do something for me and earn a bit more?"

Wouldn't we just!

He explained how every Saturday, for the next two months, he had to be up really early to catch a train to London.

"I have to be there by nine o'clock, and I won't be back again until the evening. That means poor old Dixie's going to be left by herself – and I won't be able to give her much of a walk before I go. If you two girls would take her out when you take Mud, and give her her dinner, I'd be most grateful. And, of course, I'd pay you for it!"

We would have taken Dixie out without being paid; but as it was for Warrior, we at once accepted.

"Two pounds every Saturday?" said Mr Hennessy. "Does that sound fair?"

We agreed that it did. Greatly daring, I said, "I

suppose you couldn't possibly let us have some of it in advance?"

"Like, say, about seven Saturdays' worth?" added Jilly.

"You mean, you want another fourteen pounds to make up your money?"

We nodded, breathlessly. Would he tell us we were being greedy and grasping and ungrateful and that he had changed his mind? Or would he be sympathetic and understanding?

"It is for Warrior," I said, timidly.

"We're frightened if we don't rescue him *immediately*, this beastly man will kill him!" said Jilly.

"And he's suffering," I added. "He's so unhappy!"

"Well! We can't have that," said Mr Hennessy. "I couldn't live with the reproachful looks every time I saw you. OK! If you'll get up early on Saturday and come round for Dixie before I go, I will give you your fourteen pounds. How's that?"

Oh! How I wish all men were like Mr Hennessy. Jilly and me were so excited!

"All we need now," said Jilly, "is 26p." She works these things out in her head! It's incredible.

"Twenty-six p. is *nothing*," I said.

We could rescue Warrior this coming Saturday!

Benjy came running at me when I got in. I thought he was going to start wittering on again about how he'd trained Mud to sit, or stay, or fetch. I decided that this time I would be kind and patient and let him show me. I was feeling jubilant! But guess what? It was nothing to do with Mud. It was Warrior! Benjy wanted to give me all the money out of his money box. It was just so sweet of him!

I didn't take it, of course. I might have done, if we'd needed it; but thanks to Mr Hennessy we now had enough. Well, almost.

"Just give me 26p," I said to Benjy.

"Dake *aw*," said Benjy.

"No! We don't need it all. Just 26p will do." Suddenly, money was flooding in from everywhere! "You already gave us some of your toys," I said.

Benjy perked up. "Yed, an' book!"

"And books," I agreed. "So you've helped us enormously. And when we've rescued him, we'll take you see him!"

Benjy wanted to know where Warrior would be (he thought maybe the back garden!) and this made me suddenly realize that we had never rung the horse sanctuary.

"Mum!" I said. "I'm just going round to Jilly's."

I thought that Jilly might be better than me at ringing.

Jilly thought that I would be better than her.

"You're good at talking to people!"

"But you're better at arguing!"

"I don't see why we should have to argue," said Jilly. "All you've got to do is just tell them we've rescued a horse."

Well. That is what you would think. But things just never seem to work out the way you want them to.

First off, the horse sanctuary was FULL.

Second, most of the people who took horses for them in emergencies were also FULL.

Third, they seemed to think I was about six

years old and didn't know what I was talking about.

Jilly could see that I was getting more and more frustrated. She snatched the telephone from me.

"*Please!*" she begged. "You've got to help us! This horse will die if you don't! It's got damaged lungs and they're riding it to death and we've raised all this money to rescue it and if you don't take it there's nowhere else it can go. WHAT ARE WE SUPPOSED TO DO?"

I stared at her, awestruck. I had never seen Jilly like this! I had been trying so hard to be cool and calm and reasonable, and here was Jilly practically having hysterics and it seemed that they were listening to her because suddenly she cried, "Oh, please! Please try!"

"What's happening?" I said.

"They're going to ring round all the people they know and see if they can find someone who'll take him."

"Now?"

"Tomorrow. They'll let us know."

That was another night I didn't sleep. You have

lots of sleepless nights when you're rescuing animals. There are just so many things to worry about. So many things to be upset about. Your head simply buzzes! I never tell Mum 'cos I know if I did she'd only start on about school.

"You won't be able to concentrate, Clara, if you don't have your sleep!"

It was true that next day we didn't concentrate too well. But it wasn't because of not having sleep; it was because of thinking about Warrior and what would happen to him if the sanctuary couldn't find anyone to take him.

It wasn't till Friday that our minds were set at rest. By then I'd chewed my fingers practically to stumps and Jilly had twisted her hair into so many tight little knots that she couldn't get a comb through it. Then on Friday afternoon when we got home Jilly's mum said, "Some horse person rang. A Mrs Broom. She wants you to call her."

We rang immediately! Well, Jilly did; I just listened. I didn't even have to strain my ears. Like lots of horsey people, Mrs Broom had a really LOUD sort of voice.

She said she lived in a place about three kilometres away from us called Dittington.

"Don't really have room for another horse," she barked, "but needs must. Squeeze him in. Good-natured, is he?"

Jilly said earnestly that Warrior was the gentlest, sweetest horse there ever was. Mrs Broom said, "Great! That case, no problem. Call when you've got him. I'll drive over and pick him up."

By then, Jilly was almost sobbing with relief. She tried to say thank you, but Mrs Broom cut her short.

"No need for that. All in the same business. Love horses. Can't stand cruelty. Keep it up! Doing a grand job."

It is just *such* a comfort when you come across people that think the same way you do.

Saturday morning, we set our alarms for six and went to collect Dixie. Mr Hennessy gave us our fourteen pounds, and a tin of dog food. He said, "She's had a bit of an upset tummy, so she may not eat it. The vet said not to worry if she doesn't."

We had decided that what we would do, we would take Dixie back to my place, so she wouldn't be on her own, then immediately after breakfast we would go off for our walk, with all the money that we had collected carefully tucked away in Jilly's bum bag. But instead of doing our usual walk, we would go over to Farley Down and rescue Warrior! We would take him away from that horrible place and give him to lovely Mrs Broom. We thought that having two big fierce-looking dogs with us would be a wise precaution as it would stop old Chisel becoming violent.

It seemed like a really good idea. But oh, it all went disastrously wrong! We were about half way there when poor Dixie started to droop. She put her tail between her legs and began making those horrible heavings that dogs do when they want to be sick. The trouble was, she *couldn't* be sick because she had her muzzle on.

We didn't know what to do! She wasn't allowed out without her muzzle. It was against the law.

"But she'll choke!" said Jilly.

I see now that what we *should* have done was take her muzzle off but put her on the lead. What we actually did was just take her muzzle off. We didn't think! It was our fault. We panicked. Of course, we weren't to know that a cat would choose that *precise* moment to jump out in front of us. It sprang out of the bushes and went scudding off towards its garden. It doesn't alter the fact that we should still have had Dixie on the lead. You can't make excuses for yourself if you're an Animal Lover. You have to accept responsibility.

The dogs went mad! Dixie forgot all about wanting to be sick. All she could think of was *chase-the-cat*! Before we could grab them, both she and Mud had gone streaking off in hot pursuit.

The cat dived through its garden gate; Mud and Dixie dived after it. And then the door opened and a woman appeared. The cat shot past her into the safety of its home. Mud and Dixie would have shot after it, but fortunately the woman pulled the door to and stopped them.

"I'm ever so sorry!" I panted, as Jilly and I came pounding up.

"So you should be," said the woman. "They could have killed my cat! What's this?" She took hold of Dixie's collar. Her eyes narrowed. "Is this a pit bull terrier?"

Maybe we should have said no. There are some people that would have done. Instead I burbled, "Yes, but she's not vicious, she wouldn't hurt anyone!"

"She likes cats," said Jilly.

"Why is she not wearing a muzzle?"

"She wanted to be sick," I said. "We just took it off, just for a minute!"

"You know, don't you," said the woman, "that if I reported this to the police she would be destroyed?"

"No!" screamed Jilly. "Please!"

"She's harmless!" I cried.

I crouched down beside her, and as if to prove what we'd been saying, Dixie whopped out her tongue and smacked a great big kiss on to my face. She couldn't have timed it better!

"Well! Maybe I'll overlook it just this once," said the woman. "But on two conditions . . . one, you never *ever* take such a chance again. I'm thinking of the dog, you understand? And two, you give me a contribution to my cat fund. Just to teach you a lesson!"

I think we would have agreed to give her whatever she demanded. Anything to protect poor Dixie!

The woman went indoors and reappeared with a collecting tin that had the words CRUMBLE DOWN CAT RESCUE on it. She held it out. Jilly fumbled in her bum bag. I saw her take out a note and stuff it into the tin. I was too mesmerized to say anything. I just wanted to grab Dixie and run!

"Thank you," said the woman. I must say, she sounded a bit surprised. "That's very generous of you!"

"What did you give her?" I hissed, as soon as we were safely out of reach.

"I don't know!" Jilly looked at me, stricken.

"Count the money!" I said. "Count the money!"

Jilly had given the Crumble Down Cat Rescue twenty pounds out of Warrior's rescue fund. . .

Chapter 8

Poor Jilly! She was so distressed. I kept telling her it wasn't her fault and that if I'd been the one holding the money I would probably have done the same. But she still blamed herself.

"I got in a panic," she wept. "I forgot all about Warrior! I was just thinking about Dixie and what would happen to her." Tears went spurting down her cheeks. "If Warrior dies it will be all because of me!"

"Well, it won't," I said, "'cos he's not going to! We're going to rescue him!"

"But how?" sobbed Jilly.

"Same way as before! Pay old Chisel his money."

"But it'll t-take ages to m-make up t-twenty p-pounds!"

"Wanna bet?" I said. "We'll have it by this afternoon. And then we'll go and rescue him!"

Jilly blotted her eyes. "Where are we g-going to g-get it from?"

"I'll find a way!"

"But h—"

"Be quiet!" I said. "I'm thinking!"

Ideas were fizzing through my head. I would take all my old clothes and all Benjy's old clothes and I would sell them, and never mind if Mum did find out and do her bits and pieces. Warrior would be safe! That was all that mattered.

Except, unfortunately, our old clothes probably wouldn't fetch anywhere near twenty pounds. Twenty pence, more like.

Think of something else.

OK, we could – we could go and sing in the shopping centre and have a cap for people to put money in!

We didn't have a cap. And we couldn't sing. They would most probably *stone* us.

Right. Well. We could —

"We could *collect* it!" I said.

"C-collect it? H-how?"

"Like the cat woman! She had a tin! That's what we'll do. We'll get a tin and we'll go into the shopping centre and we'll stand there and shake it and people will give us money. Quick!"

I tugged at Dixie's lead – she had her muzzle back on by now but we weren't taking any chances – and set off at a gallop, yelling over my shoulder to Jilly.

"Bring Mud! Hurry!"

Jilly and Mud came charging after us. We left the dogs with Mum and rushed round to Jilly's to find a suitable collecting pot. Jilly's mum was out, so there wasn't anyone there to start asking awkward questions, such as, *"What are you doing with that tin of peaches?"*

"She's got loads of peaches," said Jilly. "She'll never miss just one."

We took the top off with a special tin opener that Jilly's mum has that doesn't leave jagged edges. Then we ate the peaches (well, it seemed silly to waste them) and washed out the tin. Then we found one of those plastic lids they sell for putting on cans of dog and cat food and cut a slit in it with a thing called a Stanley knife that Jilly said her mum used for cutting carpet. Wow! Was it ever sharp! It sliced through the plastic like it was paper. A lethal weapon, if you ask me.

"Now we need some stickers," I said. "Two for us and one for the tin, so's people will know what we're collecting for."

This is the sticker we made for the tin:

HONEYPOT HORSE RESCUE

Honeypot is the name of the lane where we live.

For our own stickers, Jilly had a sudden burst of inspiration. On two large sheets of paper, in big, bold felt-tip pen, she wrote:

PLEASE HELP US RESCUE
WARRIOR
A POOR SICK HORSE

Then she took two black bin liners and stuck the paper on them, and fixed the bin liners to the front of our sweatshirts with safety pins. We were ready!

"I'll just go and tell Mum where we're going," I said.

Mum was in the kitchen, doing some ironing. I just stuck my head round the door about a quarter of a centimetre, so she couldn't see what I was wearing (you can't be too careful. I didn't want her stopping us before we'd even started) and gabbled, "We're just going in to town I haven't forgotten my bedroom I'll do it later that's a promise!" and went zooming off before she could say anything.

While we were waiting for the bus in to town, old Mrs Cherry came by. She is *really* old. She peered at my sticker and said, "I can't read it, dear. Is it for animals?"

I said, "It's for a poor sick horse," and she said, "That's all right, then," and gave us a whole load of 5p pieces! We both felt incredibly encouraged and even Jilly began to cheer up and talk about being able to rescue Warrior that same afternoon.

Then we hit the shopping centre. It was still pretty early and there weren't that many people about. We stood first in one place and then in another, rattling our tin with its 5p pieces. *Nobody* put any money in it.

"We should have made two tins," I said. "Then we could have stood in different places."

But Jilly said she would be too scared to stand by herself and that it was more noticeable if there were two of us.

"I think this is the best spot," she said. "Near the fountain."

Well! If that was the best spot, I can't imagine what the worst spot would have been like. A whole hour went by and all we'd collected was about 50p! In desperation, I started rattling the tin really hard and calling out to people as they passed.

"Help a sick horse! Please help a sick horse!"

A tiny child came wobbling over and made a simply huge display of giving us a 2p piece and then had the nerve to complain because we didn't have a "sticky thing" for it to wear!

"Honestly," grumbled Jilly, "you'd think it had given us a fortune, the way it was carrying on."

"Spoilt little beast," I said.

Next thing we knew, we had a rival. *Another* person with a tin came and stood right opposite us, the other side of the fountain!

"Cheek!" I said. "We were here first! Go and see what they're collecting for."

"You," said Jilly.

"I'm shaking the tin! Do you want to shake the tin?"

"No!" Jilly backed away, terrified.

"So go and ask them what they're doing here. Tell them to move somewhere else. This is our spot!"

Jilly reluctantly set off. She reached the girl with the tin and I saw her say something and then I saw the girl with the tin give me this cold, haughty stare as if I were a horribly icky fur ball sicked up by a cat. Then Jilly came trotting back. On the way, she suddenly stopped and peered at the fountain. I mean, really *peered*. It was like she'd never seen one before. I waved at her, impatiently.

"Well! Did you tell her?" I said.

"Yes, but she said she was official and had every right to be here."

"What a nerve! So have we. It's a free country. What's she collecting for, anyway?"

"I don't know, I forgot to look. Something boring. People, or something. Listen, you know the fountain?" said Jilly.

"What about it?"

"It's got loads of money in it."

"*Money?*"

"In the water. All coins. Just lying there."

We exchanged glances. We didn't have to say anything. We both knew what the other was thinking. *It might SEEM like stealing, but it's for Warrior. . .*

Slowly, we moved forward.

"Look, she's going!" said Jilly.

"Good! But let's do this first."

Before there were great crowds of people around. I mean, it *wasn't* stealing. Whoever had put the coins in the water must have known they would be taken out again. They had probably meant for them to go to a good cause. And if rescuing Warrior wasn't a good cause, I didn't know what was.

All the same, it seemed best not to take any

chances. We'd already had one disaster. We didn't want another!

We kind of sauntered over to the fountain, trying to make like we just needed a bit of a rest. The fountain is shaped like an enormous basin, with a rim that you can sit on. In the middle is a big stone fish, gushing water out of its mouth. And Jilly was right: in the water, there was money! Lots of it. Coins of all kinds, just lying there. Copper, mostly, but I could see a few silver ones here and there.

"Try for the pounds and fifties." I said it out of the side of my mouth, the way they sometimes do in old detective movies.

Jilly nodded. All casual, she reached behind her with one hand and dipped it in the water. I did the same. My fingers had just closed on something that felt like a 50p when I saw our rival coming back. She was with a man. He was wearing a uniform. . .

My heart sank. *Now* what?

"We're not stealing," squeaked Jilly. "Clara, tell them! We're not stealing!"

But the man didn't seem to have noticed that

we were fishing for coins in the fountain. He seemed more interested in our collecting pot.

"You kids," he said. "What do you think you're doing? This is private property! You have no right to collect money on these premises unless you have a permit. Which you have not got."

How did he know?

He knew because he was a security guard. I'd heard about security guards. Darren Bickerstaff had told me. They could arrest you on the spot!

"We were just trying to get some money to help a poor sick horse," I stammered.

"Well, you go elsewhere and do it. Not in here."

"They're not allowed, anyway!" screeched the girl with the tin. "They're under age! It's illegal!"

That was when we really drooped. It was like all the stuffing had been knocked out of us. Whatever we tried to do, it seemed there were laws against it. We couldn't hold a raffle, we couldn't collect, we weren't even supposed to have gone on our sponsored walk. I think we both felt utterly dejected.

And then something happened that I can only describe as *a miracle*. This lady was walking past. We didn't recognize her at first – but she recognized us! She stopped and said, "Oh, dear! In trouble *again*?"

It was the cat lady! The one Jilly had given our twenty pounds to!

"What's the problem this time?" she said.

Miserably, I explained how we were trying to collect money to rescue Warrior.

"We thought we'd make a tin like your cat one, but they won't let us!"

"They won't let us do *anything*," said Jilly.

"Whatever we try, they say it's illegal!"

"Alas," said the cat lady, "that is bewrockrissy for you."

Well, that is what I *thought* she said. I have since discovered that it is spelt b.u.r.e.a.u.c.r.a.c.y. What it means is, rules and regulations and people telling you you cannot do things.

"Making money is never easy."

"We had enough before Dixie got sick!" I didn't mean to sound accusing, but Jilly immediately burst into tears and cried, "Oh,

Clara, don't! Warrior's going to die and it's all my fault!"

The cat lady said, "Why is it all your fault?"

"It's not," I said. "It's both our faults."

Before I knew it, I was telling the cat lady the whole sad story.

"And then Dixie wanted to be sick, so we took her muzzle off—"

"And I gave you twenty pounds 'cos I was in a panic and now we don't have enough left!" The tears came bubbling up in Jilly's eyes all over again. They were already red from the crying she'd done earlier.

"I see!" The cat lady nodded. "I'm beginning to get the picture. I wondered why you were so generous! I only meant you to put 50p in the pot. I just wanted to teach you a lesson. Not rob you!"

"We robbed Warrior," sobbed Jilly. "We've robbed him of his life!"

"Now, now, don't be over-dramatic." The cat lady said it briskly. She was quite a brisk sort of person. "All is not yet lost! Where exactly is he, this horse of yours?"

I told her that he was at Farley Down, and she raised her eyebrows.

"That place! It should have been closed years ago. So, they're flogging this poor animal to death but if you can manage to raise enough money you can rescue him. Only now you're twenty pounds short. Well! You've got yourselves in a right pickle, haven't you?"

We nodded, glumly.

"What is the solution? Suppose you give me what you've got in that tin, and in return I give you your twenty pounds back. How does that strike you?"

Jilly said, "Oh!" and clapped her hands to her mouth. I think she just couldn't believe it. Someone was being *nice* to us!

I said "Oh" as well. But instead of clapping my hands to my mouth, I thrust our tin at the cat lady. "That means we could and rescue him straight away!"

"How do you propose to get there?" said the cat lady. "It's a fair distance. Would you like me to drive you?"

Better and better! Sometimes you feel that there *is* some justice in the world.

But Jilly was plucking at me.

"C-Clara . . . you don't think—"

"What?"

"We ought to ring home?"

I was about to say *no* – I just wanted to get to Warrior – when the cat lady stepped in.

"Certainly you ought! You should always ring home. Go and do it right away."

I pulled a face at Jilly. Her and her stupid ideas! It was all wasting valuable time. And in any case, as it happened, neither of our mums were in, so we had to leave a message on my mum's answerphone.

"At least it will stop them worrying," said Jilly.

Yes, I thought, and Warrior could be *dead*. But I didn't say so. Jilly was already feeling quite guilty enough.

We all set off in the cat lady's car. It had cat stickers all over it – Cats' Protection League, and Crumble Down Cat Rescue – and smelt a bit catty in a nice, cosy sort of way.

The lady's name was Miss Hatterman and as it

turned out it was just as well she was with us. I don't know what we'd have done if she hadn't been. We might even have given up. I *hope* we wouldn't, but we were just feeling so bruised and battered.

When we got to the stables Miss Hatterman said she had better come in with us, "Just in case". I think she meant just in case old Chisel tried to chisel us – which is exactly what he did.

For a start, Warrior wasn't there. He'd been sent on another hack. . .

Jilly clutched at my arm. I could feel her fingers, digging into me.

"I thought, according to these young girls," said Miss Hatterman, "this particular horse was not fit to be taken on hacks?"

"These two young girls ought to mind their own poxy business!" snarled old Chisel. "Aside from anything else, they haven't the faintest idea what they're talking about!"

"Well, there's a perfectly easy way to find out," said Miss Hatterman. "We can always call a vet to come and examine the horse. See what he says."

"You do that," agreed old Chisel. "He'll tell

you what I'm telling you ... that horse is as fit as any other horse so long as it's ridden quietly."

"He wasn't ridden quietly last time!" I cried. "He came back all in a lather!"

"Yes, and he was being *cantered*," said Jilly. "We saw him!"

"Did you, now?"

"Yes, we did! And he shouldn't be! He's got damaged lungs!"

Jilly turned, desperately, to Miss Hatterman. We were terrified that she would choose to believe old Chisel rather than us. Grown-ups almost always side with each other against young people. But Miss Hatterman obviously didn't like old Chisel – well, I don't really see how anyone could, the way he kept shouting four-letter words all over the place.

"I believe you agreed that if these girls could raise sufficient money, you would let them take the horse away."

"I might have done. Might not have done."

"Did you, or didn't you?" said Miss Hatterman.

"What if I did?"

"We've got the money!" Jilly went to open her bag, but Miss Hatterman put out a hand to stop her.

"Not until we see the horse."

"Well, you can't see the horse, 'cos it's not poxy well here! What do you think I am? A poxy magician? In any case, I've changed my mind. You can keep your money. I'll keep the horse."

Old Chisel went striding off, all bow-legged and belligerent, across the yard.

"You can't do this!" I screamed. "We had an agreement!"

"Agreement? You think I give a toss for some poxy agreement?" Old Chisel turned and made a rude sign. A *really* rude sign. "Get out of my poxy yard!"

"Charming," murmured Miss Hatterman.

"We *did* have an agreement," I said.

"Oh, I believe you! Don't worry. I'm on your side. Let us see –" Miss Hatterman beckoned imperiously to a girl who had just emerged from one of the boxes – "if we can prise out a bit more information."

The girl came up. She wasn't much older than us and she was looking really scared.

"It's all right, I'm not going to eat you," said Miss Hatterman. But I don't think it was Miss Hatterman she was scared of; I think it was old Chisel. "We'd just like to know where the ride has gone."

The girl cast a fearful glace back over her shoulder.

"Gone to the Gallops," she muttered.

The Gallops! My heart sank, like a lead weight. Everyone – unless they were beginners – took the Gallops at full tilt.

"Oh, no," whispered Jilly. She had turned sheet white. For just a moment, I really thought she was going to faint.

"Come!" Miss Hatterman led the way back to the car. "Let us go and intercept them!"

Miss Hatterman was quite old – at least seventy, I should think – but she drove that car like she was Michael Schumacher, or someone.

As we reached the Gallops, we could see the ride strung out along its length. Even those poor knackered horses from Farley Down were flogged at full stretch along the Gallops.

"Where's your one?" said Miss Hatterman. "Can you see him?"

"N-no," said Jilly. Then, "*Yes!* He's right up at the front!"

The big red-faced man was riding him. He had a crop, and he was thrashing Warrior with it, to make him go.

Jilly screamed. I stuffed my fist in my mouth.

Miss Hatterman, grim-faced, said, "We'll put a stop to this!"

She stepped on the gas and the car shot down the road that ran alongside. We soon overtook the horses. But even as we drew to a halt, Warrior stumbled and fell.

He did not get up again.

We were too late.

Chapter 9

Miss Hatterman brought the car to a stop. Jilly and I went stumbling out.

"Warrior!" I cried. "Oh, Warrior!"

I fell to my knees beside him. That poor, gentle, trusting horse – killed by the greed and cruelty of human beings!

Jilly knelt down next to me. Tears were streaming from her eyes.

The red-faced man had come off when Warrior fell. He had gone sprawling. Serves him right! Maybe he had broken his neck. Who cared?

Warrior was all we cared about! Our dear, sweet, darling Warrior. He'd already suffered so much in his life! Caught in a fire, terrified and unable to escape. He should have been allowed to live out his remaining years in a lush green meadow, with friends. Not ridden to death by some horrible brute of a man, thrashing at him, terrorizing him, digging his heels into him.

All the other riders had pulled up. They sat there, white-faced, staring at that big, brave, beautiful horse lying so still on the ground. Natalie was the only one who dismounted. She handed the reins to someone and came over.

"We told you!" sobbed Jilly. "We told you!"

The red-faced man had picked himself up.

"I wasn't to know! How was I to know? Jeff said he was OK! He said he was just lazy. How was I to know?"

I opened my mouth to yell something – I'm not sure what I was going to yell. "You idiot!" or "Murderer!" Something like that. But Jilly gasped, "Clara!" and tugged at my sleeve. I looked down. Warrior was still alive! His eyes had opened and his flanks had started to heave as he struggled for breath.

Jilly and me crouched there, murmuring to him, urgently but softly, so that only he could hear.

"Darling Warrior! Please don't die! We love

you so much! We've fought so hard! Please, Warrior! Stay with us!"

Of course we knew he couldn't understand us. But he was a poor sick animal in distress and all we could hope was that the sound of our voices, whispering in his ear, and the feel of our hands, gently stroking and soothing, would bring him some comfort and give him the will to go on fighting.

I don't know what Natalie was doing all this time. Just standing there, I guess; I didn't bother to look. I was too concerned with our poor Warrior, trying to ease his suffering.

After what seemed like ages, but in fact was probably only a few minutes, Warrior started to make feeble attempts to get back on his feet. We didn't know whether to help him or try and keep him still. If he wanted to get up, then surely that must be a good sign?

But suppose the strain proved too much?

We didn't know what to do!

It was Miss Hatterman who came to our aid. Not Natalie, who should have been the one. After all, she was in charge of the ride. She was supposed to know about horses. But she just stood there, looking dazed. As if for the first time she was accepting that everything we'd told her had been true. Warrior *did* have damaged lungs and he *shouldn't* have been ridden.

Miss Hatterman said, "Easy, now! Take it easy, boy!" And then she helped us – ever so gently – to get Warrior back up. It seemed to be what he wanted to do. They say that animals know what is best for themselves, the way that dogs, for instance, will eat grass if they are feeling sick, so maybe you have to let them choose.

"Where was it you were planning to take him?" said Miss Hatterman.

We told her that we had to telephone Mrs Broom and she would come with her horsebox and fetch him.

"Do you have Mrs Broom's number?"

I looked at Jilly, appalled. What had we done with it? Fortunately, Jilly has the sort of brain that can remember things like telephone numbers. She reeled it off without a moment's hesitation.

"Right!" Miss Hatterman reached into her car and whipped out a mobile phone. I was dead impressed! For an old lady, she was really clued in. My mum doesn't even have a mobile.

"I'll ask her to come over straight away."

Natalie suddenly sprang back to life. She said, "Excuse me, this horse belongs to my father."

Miss Hatterman regarded her, coldly. "In that case, young woman, your father should be ashamed of himself. He'll be lucky if he doesn't face a prosecution."

That shut her up!

By now, all the other riders had dismounted and were standing around in a little huddle. Red Face was still explaining, to anyone who would listen, that it wasn't his fault: "Jeff said he was OK!"

It was true that old Chisel *had* tried making out that Warrior was fit enough to be ridden, so maybe I should have felt at least a little bit sorry for poor old Red Face. I should think it would haunt you all your life long, knowing that you have flogged and whipped and beaten a noble animal almost to its death. But all my sympathies were with Warrior; I didn't have any to spare for the person who had caused him such agony.

Jilly and I stood one on either side of him, as he struggled for breath. His ears were pulled back, his lips stretched over his teeth, and his poor eyes were rolling in their sockets. Horrid foamy stuff was coming out of his nostrils, and his flanks were heaving with the effort of trying to get enough air into his lungs. He was trembling all over, and the sweat was pouring off him.

I said to Natalie, "He'll get cold! We should wipe him!"

Natalie just shook her head, helplessly, as if to say, "What with?" I think she cared, sort of. But she was just so shocked by what had happened. She had this almost glazed expression in her eyes. Perhaps because she hadn't realized until now how cruel and grasping her dad really was.

Warrior suddenly threw his head into the air, then let it sink back down again between his shoulders.

"Let's take his saddle off," said Jilly.

That was a good idea, and one that I should have thought of. We removed the saddle, and the saddle-blanket, as well, because it was drenched through with sweat. We had to find something to wipe him with!

"Here," said Miss Hatterman. "Put this over him."

She had taken a rug from the car; a lovely warm tartan rug! We draped it over him, and then I had an idea of my own. I tore off my sweatshirt, and the T-shirt that I had underneath, and I used the T-shirt for wiping off some of the sweat. I didn't care that everyone was watching! Usually I am rather modest (Mum says I am *bashful*) but I would have done anything to help that poor trembling boy.

After a few seconds, Jilly followed suit. She took off her T-shirt, as well. And all those riders just stood there and gawked! The trouble was, they weren't really horse people. No real horse person would ever ride at a stable like Farley Down. They were people who just came out for the occasional hack; they probably didn't even put their own saddles and bridles on. They didn't know the first thing about horses.

Well, Jilly and me didn't know a whole lot more, but at least we were trying. At least we *cared*.

"How is he?" said Miss Hatterman. She took hold of Warrior's bridle and gently stroked his neck. "Poor boy! You're very distressed, aren't you? Don't worry! We'll soon have you tucked into a nice cosy stall and the vet will come and see you."

It is so lovely when a grown up person talks to animals the way that me and Jilly do! Most grown ups are too embarrassed; they think it makes them look silly. It didn't worry Miss Hatterman! I expect she talked to her cats like that.

"Your Mrs Broom is on her way," she said. "She'll be here in a few minutes."

You will simply never guess what happened next. There was a loud screech of brakes and a car pulled up. It was old Chisel! He came roaring over, waving his arms like a windmill and screaming four-letter words, a great long spew of them.

"What the devil is going on here? What have you done to my poxy horse? And what are you poxy kids doing?"

"They're taking him to a sanctuary." That was

Natalie. She sounded quite defiant. I couldn't believe it! Suddenly, she was on our side! "They've got someone coming to take him away."

"My **** horse?" screamed old Chisel. "That's my **** horse!"

Sometimes people's language is so bad you just *have* to put stars.

Miss Hatterman had stepped forward, protectively, between us and old Chisel. "It is not your horse," she said. "We are removing it from you. And if you give us any trouble, we shall bring a prosecution."

Old Chisel had gone so purple in the face, I thought he was going to explode. Either that, or give Miss Hatterman a black eye. And then a surprising thing happened. The red-faced man came running over. He grabbed hold of old Chisel's collar and began shaking him, to and fro.

"You told me that horse was fit to be ridden! You gave me your word! You said if it didn't go, then to give it some stick. You said it was just lazy. Now look at it! Look at the state of it!"

He lifted old Chisel off the ground and swung

him round, like a puppet, so that he was forced to look at Warrior.

"Collapsed, didn't it? With me on top of it! I could have broken my neck!"

"Yes, and the horse could have died!" That was another of the riders, deciding to join in. A woman. "You must have known it wasn't fit!"

"He had no right sending it out like that!"

"Shouldn't be allowed to keep horses if that's the way he treats them!"

They were all at it now; all ganging up on old Chisel. I was glad! It was about time. He didn't run a stables, he ran a prison. All his horses were knackered. They weren't fed properly, they weren't kept properly, and now he'd almost managed to kill our poor Warrior.

A horsebox had drawn up behind Miss Hatterman's car. A big, plump woman wearing a fat sweater and tight, stretchy riding breeches got out of it and came running over.

"This the horse? Let me look at him! Oh, my poor baby! You poor, poor baby! What have they been doing to you?"

"Riding him to death!" I said.

"Yes! It looks like it."

She ran her hands over Warrior's trembling flanks. You could just tell, from the way she did it, that she knew about horses.

"Will he be all right?" whispered Jilly.

"Get him back to my place. Already rung the vet. Should be there to meet us."

Gently, step by faltering step, she coaxed Warrior towards the horsebox. Old Chisel didn't say a word. Not even a four-letter one! Some of the riders were muttering about reporting him to the RSPCA. Even his own daughter wouldn't speak up for him. Old Chisel had had his day!

We helped lead Warrior up the ramp – he was still rather wobbly, but he was so brave! Mrs Broom said that if we liked we could stay with him. She said it would help calm him if we were there.

We remembered, just in time, to call out our thanks to Miss Hatterman for all that she'd done.

"Ring me," she said. "Let me know what happens."

We promised that we would.

All the way to Mrs Broom's place we talked to

Warrior in what we hoped were soothing tones. Jilly remembered what Christy had once told us, about how you could communicate with horses by gently blowing up their nostrils. She tried it with Warrior, and I think he liked it because he twitched an ear. I kept stroking him, trying to stop him trembling, trying to reassure him that nothing else bad was going to happen to him. I was terrified he might think that he was going to the knacker's yard. It made me go cold all over to reflect that this was almost certainly what would have happened if Jilly and me – and Miss Hatterman – hadn't turned up when we did.

The vet was already there, waiting for us, as we drove into Mrs Broom's yard. Mrs Broom said that as Warrior knew us, we should be the ones to introduce him to his new home. We made it as easy for him as we possibly could, murmuring words of encouragement every step of the way. He was so good, and so docile! All he wanted to do – all he'd ever wanted to do – was just to please people.

He was still trembling, though not quite as badly as before, but he obviously knew we were trying to help him. We took his bridle, Jilly on one side, me on the other, and we walked him ever so slowly across the yard and into the big airy box, sweet-smelling, with a bed of fresh straw, that had been prepared for him.

We would have given anything to be able to stay until the vet had finished, but Mrs Broom warned us that he might be there some time. She said, "He's a very sick horse. It won't be quick or easy. But rest assured, I'll call you the minute there's any news."

With that, sadly, we had to be content. We kissed Warrior goodbye and set off on the long journey home. We had to take a bus as far as Crumble Down, and then walk back across the fields. Of course, Mum was in a state, wondering what had happened. (GIRLS MUGGED IN SHOPPING PRECINCT. . .) She said, "I got your message but you've been gone for hours!"

"We had to rescue Warrior," I said. "And I haven't forgotten about my bedroom, I'll do it straight away, I promise!"

But Mum didn't seem so fussed about my bedroom; she wanted to know about Warrior.

When she heard that he was safe with Mrs Broom she heaved a great sigh of relief and said, "Now, maybe, life can return to normal!" And then she added, "Whatever passes for normal, with you two. This week a horse, next week, who knows? A hippopotamus?"

We *would* rescue a hippopotamus. Of course we would! If we ever came across one that was in trouble.

I'd just finished tidying my bedroom when the telephone rang. It was Jilly. She said, "Mrs Broom just called. Warrior's going to be all right!"

"Hey! Wow! Yikes!" I jumped up and punched the air. Our big boy was safe!

"She said we can go and see him whenever we want, maybe next Saturday, and do you want to ring Miss Hatterman or shall I do it?"

I said that I would do it as I really like giving good news to people. I had to look her up in the telephone book as we didn't have her number, but fortunately Hatterman is not a very common name. In fact, she was the only one!

Miss Hatterman seemed almost as pleased as me and Jilly.

"Splendid!" she said. "Absolutely splendid! Now, whatever you do, don't give a penny piece to that man. *Not one penny piece.* Do you hear me?"

It was only then that I remembered . . . we had one hundred and fifty pounds that we didn't need any more! I rang Jilly back immediately and we discussed what to do with it. We decided it was only right it should go to Mrs Broom, for looking after Warrior.

We agreed that we would take it over the following Saturday, in the morning, before we went for our ride. We had to take the dogs out first, of course; and I *was* supposed to tidy my bedroom.

"But we have to go and see Warrior," I said to Mum. "I'll do it the minute I get back . . . I promise, I promise!"

"Before you go riding," said Mum.

"Yes, yes!" I said. "Before I go riding!"

Jilly and me were so happy, sitting on the bus on our way to see Warrior. I just don't know *how* we managed to get into a row with each other. I mean, we never have rows! We're above all that sort of thing. We are Animal Lovers, and animals come first. We don't have time for bickering and squabbling.

I can't remember which of us started it. It may have been Jilly; it may have been me. I think I said something about having to tidy my bedroom before we went for our ride, and Jilly pointed out that we hadn't actually booked for a ride.

I said, "No, but they'll be expecting us. I mean, we always go on a Saturday."

Except when we went on a Sunday.

Jilly said, "We didn't go last Saturday. *Or* the Saturday before. We went to old Chisel's."

"Hmm! Yes," I said. "I'd better ring them as soon as we get back."

After that there was a bit of a silence, then Jilly suddenly burst out, "I'm not sure we ought to be doing it!"

"Doing what?" I said.

"*Riding,*" said Jilly.

That was how it started. But whether it was my fault or Jilly's that we ended up being so foul to each other, I am not really sure.

I remember Jilly saying that riding was OK if you owned your own horse, because then you could be sure it was being looked after and not ridden to death or kept in a horrible dark prison cell. Also, she said, it wouldn't be sent for horse meat if it got sick, or sold to someone else if you grew too big for it.

I remember saying that I agreed with her, but that if people like us didn't go riding at riding schools there wouldn't *be* any riding schools, and then what would happen to all the poor horses?

Jilly then said something about too many horses being bred, anyway – "Half of them end up as horse meat" – and I said, "Well, *all* of them would end up as horse meat if you had your way!"

Jilly then accused me of not caring about the welfare of horses but only about my own selfish enjoyment.

"Just because you like riding, you try to pretend it's all right!"

Well! That made me pretty furious, as you can imagine. So in return I told her that she only wanted to stop because she didn't really enjoy it.

"Because basically you're scared!"

I suppose it was rather disgusting of me. But she had accused me of being selfish!

After that, it all went to pieces. By the time we reached Mrs Broom's we were hardly on speaking terms. But then we saw Warrior, our brave, darling, beautiful boy! And all our anger just melted away.

You *can't* be mad at each other when you both love animals. It is just such a waste of energy.

Warrior was in his box, standing there with his big horsey head hanging over the top of the door. When he saw us, his ears pricked up and he made a little excited whinnying sound.

"He recognizes us!" cried Jilly.

"Well, of course he does," said Mrs Broom. "Horses aren't stupid! They always remember their friends."

We gave him some lovely juicy apples that we'd brought, and we cuddled him and crooned over him, and he rubbed his head against us and did his old tricks of nuzzling our pockets with his nose. He knew that was where we used to carry titbits! And of course we'd put some in there, just in case. I had a carrot and Jilly had a biscuit.

It was so heart-warming! He was looking like his old self again. His head was up, his coat was shiny, he was interested in all that was going on around him. He still trusted human beings and wanted to please them, in spite of all that he had suffered.

"But you won't ever suffer again," I whispered.

Mrs Broom said that next week she would turn him into the paddock with her other rescues.

"He'll lead the good life from now on."

We gave her the money we'd collected and she was ever so grateful. It made it seem all worth while! We forgot all the horrid things that had happened. Old Chisel swearing at us, and the security guard threatening us, and the angry women who'd thought we were trying to steal their shopping trolleys. Our big, brave, beautiful boy was safe, and that was all that mattered.

It's moments like that when you know you'll always fight for animals. You'll go on rescuing them, no matter what. Once you've started, it's impossible to stop.

We said our goodbyes to our Brave Warrior. Jilly blew up his nose and kissed him; I wobbled his big rubbery lip with my finger. We promised that we would come back and visit him.

"Though I expect," said Jilly, "he'll find himself a lady love and forget all about us."

"He may well find a lady love," agreed Mrs Broom, "but he'll never forget you."

Jilly and I set off back down the lane, towards the bus-stop. We were silent for a while, then suddenly we both spoke together.

"I'm ever so s—"

"I'm really s—"

We stopped.

"After you."

We said that together, too!

"I'm really sorry I said that you were scared," I said.

"I'm sorry I said that you were selfish," said Jilly.

"Well, but I probably am." I sighed. This was a BIG DECISION I was about to take. "You're right, I'm just thinking about me. Not the horses. We'll have to stop doing it."

"Oh, but Clara, that's not fair!" said Jilly. "You'll miss it far more than I will!"

"Right!" I leapt into the air and snatched at the overhanging branches of a tree. "That means I'm

157

making a huge big MEGA sacrifice! And you're only making a small one!"

"I am," said Jilly, sounding all humble.

"Heavens, I was only *joking*," I said.

Jilly linked her arm through mine.

"When we're grown up and we've got our own sanctuary, you can ride all you like. 'Cos they'll be *our* horses and we'll know they're loved and looked after."

"Yes, and this afternoon," I said, "*when* I've tidied my bedroom, we could go into town and have a mooch round."

It would be a relief, after all the hard work we'd put in, to be able to just saunter and stroll without having to rack our brains how to rescue some poor ill-used animal.

I said this to Jilly and she said, "Yes – until the next time! After all, we are Animal Lovers. We have to be on the look out."

You bet! We always are.